PRAISE FOR
THE TEMPTATION SAGA

"Is it hot in here? Congratulations, Ms. Hardt. You dropped me into the middle of a scorching hot story and let me burn."
~ Seriously Reviewed

"I took this book to bed with me and I didn't sleep until 4 a.m. Yes, it's that damn engrossing, so grab your copy now!"
~Whirlwind Books

"Temptation never tasted so sweet... Both tempting, and a treasure... this book held many of the seductive vices I've come to expect from Ms. Hardt's work."
~Bare Naked Words

Teasing
ANNIE

THE TEMPTATION SAGA
BOOK TWO

WATERHOUSE PRESS

Teasing

ANNIE

THE TEMPTATION SAGA
BOOK TWO

For my sons, Eric and Grant McConnell.
I'm so proud of both of you!

CHAPTER ONE

Dallas McCray was a little bit in love with his brother's wife.

Not in an "I have to have you" kind of way—though if they were both unattached he wouldn't kick Dusty out of bed—but more in an "I really wish I had someone like you to share my life with" kind of way.

He couldn't help thinking about his brother's happy marriage as he stared at the manila envelope he had just pulled from his mailbox.

His final divorce papers.

He took a deep breath and tore open the package. There it was in black-and-white. His marriage was over.

Not that he was upset about it. He no longer loved Chelsea. He wasn't sure he ever had, at least not in the way that Zach and Dusty loved each other. But failure was difficult for Dallas. Even the failure of a marriage he no longer wanted sliced like a hunting knife into his gut.

He strode into his home office, rolling his eyes at the thought of the colossal financial settlement he had paid Chelsea. Anything to keep from having to pay her alimony. He wanted her out of his life for good.

A clean break.

It had been easy enough. For Chelsea, it had always been about the money, and Dallas had plenty.

Thank God they hadn't had kids. Another knife cut into Dallas's heart at the thought of children. He had wanted them.

Chelsea hadn't. His face tensed at the memories of how she had deceived him.

Quickly he shoved the divorce papers into a file drawer. Best to get them out of sight.

So he didn't have children. Perhaps it wasn't meant to be. He was glad he hadn't had them with Chelsea, or he'd be bound to her for eternity. He'd probably be a terrible father anyway. His younger brothers had hated him growing up. They'd seen him only as an overbearing control freak, and he hadn't been close to either one. He was only now making reparations for his past actions toward them. Thankfully, they were both open to a new relationship with him.

On a whim, he picked up his cell phone and called Zach.

"What's up, Dallas?"

"They came today."

"The papers? You all right?"

"Yeah. I'm fine."

"Why don't you come to the house for dinner tonight? You shouldn't be alone."

"Nah. I'm okay."

"Come on. You know how Dusty loves to fuss over people. And Seanie misses his Uncle Dallas."

Dallas grinned as he thought of his one-year-old nephew. He did love that little guy, and letting Dusty fuss over him didn't sound too bad either.

"Deal," he said to Zach. "What time?"

"How's six-thirty sound? Seraphina's making spaghetti."

"Great." Dallas's mouth watered at the thought of zesty marinara. Zach and Dusty's housekeeper's Italian cuisine was legendary. "See you then."

★ ★ ★

Annie DeSimone yawned, stretching her bare arms over her head, her silver bangle bracelets clinking in her ears. Her first week as the new veterinarian in the small ranching town of Bakersville, Colorado was nearing its end, and already she had treated five horses, three cows, a stubborn bull, two dogs, and had delivered a litter of eight kittens.

To top it off, her VW Beetle had died on the way back from her last call, and she'd had to hitch a ride back to her office. Not a stellar first week, though at least the busyness had kept her mind off of other things.

Although it was only four, an hour before closing time, she walked to the door to lock up. As she flipped the sign from open to closed, a young woman walked around from the small parking lot behind the office, carrying a small child on one hip and an orange-and-white cat on the other.

"Geez," Annie said under her breath. She pasted a smile on her exhausted face and opened the door. "Hi," she said to the woman.

"You must be the new vet."

"Yes. I'm Dr. Annie DeSimone. Call me Annie. And you are?"

"Dusty McCray." She motioned to the pretty little boy who had striking light blue eyes and his mama's reddish-blond hair. "This is my son, Sean, and this"—she held up the cat—"is Nigel."

"It's nice to meet all of you," Annie said. She stroked Nigel's soft fur. "What seems to be the problem with Nigel today?"

"He's been lethargic for a few days," Dusty said. "Today,

though, he wouldn't eat anything at all, and his belly seems a little swollen. I think he might have a bowel obstruction." Dusty smiled nervously. "I'm afraid he likes to eat plastic wrap. We try to keep him away from it, but..."

"No need to explain. There's no keeping a curious cat from what he wants. The saying had to come from somewhere didn't it?"

"Saying?"

"Curiosity killed the cat, of course."

Dusty let out a small giggle. "I suppose so."

"But don't worry. Nigel's curiosity is only a small setback. Let's get him back on the table and have a look." Annie took the cat from his owner and led them to a small examining room. "All right, buddy, let's see what's going on." She set the cat down on the table and began her examination. "Has he vomited at all?"

"No," Dusty said.

"Any diarrhea?"

"Not that I've seen."

Annie palpated the cat's belly. "There's some distention here," she said, "but nothing too drastic. I don't think it's an obstruction. I think he may have eaten something that didn't agree with him."

Dusty sighed. "Yes, that's possible. The silly thing gets into everything."

Annie laughed. "Some cats are like that. If it would make you feel better, I can do a quick x-ray to definitely rule out an obstruction."

"Would you mind? Nigel is really special to me. I don't want to take any chances with him."

"Not at all. I'll need you to hold him down." She handed

Dusty a lead apron. "Is there any chance you might be pregnant?"

"No."

Annie showed Dusty how to position Nigel. "How would you like to come into the next room with me?" she asked Sean. "You can push the button."

Sean smiled and went willingly. *What a sweet little boy.*

After they had taken the picture, she took Sean back to his mother. "Why don't the two of you sit down out front and I'll be out in a few minutes. You can take Nigel with you."

Dusty nodded and led her son away.

Annie studied the digital image of the cat's abdomen. No obstruction, but he was a little constipated. Unusual for a cat, but not unheard of. She headed out front.

"Good news," she said. "As I suspected, there is no obstruction. He's a little backed up, though."

"Backed up?"

"Constipated."

"Oh." Dusty giggled. "I didn't know that could happen to cats."

"It can happen to any living creature," Annie said. "I'm going to give him a mild stool softener, and I suggest you keep him outside as much as you can for the next few days."

"Yes, of course."

"Don't hesitate to call if he gets worse," Annie said.

"I won't. Thank you so much. I know you were getting ready to close when I got here, and I really appreciate your time."

"No problem. I'm usually open till five, and of course I'm always on call for emergencies." She yawned. "It's been a harrowing week, though, and yes, I was tempted to close up early. But I'm glad I got to meet you and Sean and Nigel." She smiled.

"Have you met many people yet?"

"Only those whose animals I've treated. I've been hopping since I opened on Monday."

"Would you like to come to my house tonight for dinner?" Dusty asked. "It would give me a chance to repay you for your kindness, and I'd love for you to meet my husband."

A home-cooked meal sounded wonderful to Annie, who had subsisted on Lean Cuisines since she had opened up shop. "I'd love to come, but unfortunately my car died earlier today. I had it towed to Joe's down the street. I'm afraid I'm without transportation. Maybe some other time?"

"Don't be silly," Dusty said. "You can drive home with me right now, and Zach can drive you home later."

"I don't want to impose."

"You're not imposing. I'm the one who imposed on you late on a Friday afternoon when you were clearly trying to cut out early. Please. It would mean a lot to me."

"You're sure your husband won't mind?"

"Of course not."

"Well, then, I have to tell you, a home-cooked meal sounds absolutely divine."

"You'll love Seraphina's spaghetti," Dusty said. "Let's go." The pretty young woman offered a wide smile, which Annie returned.

She had made her first friend in Bakersville.

★ ★ ★

As Dusty pulled her minivan into the long driveway, Annie

stared in awe at the sprawling ranch house. This was McCray Landing, the largest and most profitable ranch in southeastern Colorado. She had been so exhausted earlier that she hadn't made the connection with Dusty's last name. Zach McCray was the middle brother and the only married one, according to the gossip she had heard.

"Here we are," Dusty said, engaging the parking brake. "Home sweet home."

"I'll say," Annie said. "It's beautiful."

She opened the car door and looked around while Dusty unstrapped Sean from his car seat.

"Mama," Sean said, as Dusty scooped him up.

"Can you take Nigel?" she asked Annie.

"Sure." Annie cradled the cat in her arms.

"This way," Dusty said, and led Annie up the narrow sidewalk and into the house.

Straight out of *House Beautiful*. Annie widened her eyes as she took in the elegant surroundings. Jade marble tile graced the entryway. Off to the right was a large living room with maple hardwood floors and a deep red plush oriental rug. A black lacquer grand piano stood in the corner, flanked by a black-and-crimson satin sofa and two wingback chairs. Mahogany coffee and end tables completed the picture.

Annie hoped they wouldn't sit in there. She was afraid she'd tarnish the perfection of the room.

Dusty led her to a different room. A rustic, cozy family area in the back of the house. Hardwood floors again, but this time with brown leather furniture and a bear skin rug next to a cozy hearth. Annie winced a little at the bear skin. She didn't like animal trophies.

"It's fake," Dusty said.

"Oh, I didn't mean—"

"It's okay. You're a vet. You wouldn't be a vet if you didn't love animals. I'm the same way."

"Oh?"

"Yeah. I always wanted to be a vet, but I wasn't able to finish college due to...circumstances."

"Have you considered going back and finishing now?" Annie asked. "You seem to know a lot about animals. Most people wouldn't have suspected a bowel obstruction with Nigel today."

"I was never able to swing it," Dusty said. "Then I met Zach and had Sean, and I don't really have any desire to go back to school now."

"I understand," Annie said, and she did. A child and husband to love meant everything.

"I wanted to get rid of the rug," Dusty continued, pointing to the bearskin. "Even a fake one bothers me a bit. But Zach wouldn't hear of it. It was his father's."

"I see."

"You get used to it after a while. Seanie loves to sit on it. It's really soft. Here, feel."

Annie smiled. "I'll take your word for it."

"I understand." Dusty smiled, her brown eyes crinkling. "Would you like something to drink? We're having spaghetti, so red wine would be nice."

Annie inhaled deeply. "I smelled the sauce when we walked in. I love Italian. I *am* Italian, actually."

"I thought so, from your last name." Dusty smiled. "Maybe you can give Seraphina some pointers."

"Seraphina is..."

"Our housekeeper," Dusty said. "But she loves to cook so

she does a lot of that as well. Zach wanted to hire a full-time cook but I said no. I love Seraphina's cooking, and when she doesn't cook, I do."

"That's nice," Annie said. What else could she say? Having the kind of money to hire not only a housekeeper but also a full-time cook was a completely foreign concept to her. "But I don't think she needs any pointers. It smells wonderful."

"You'll love it. So what do you want to drink?"

Before Annie could answer, two men walked in the back door, rustling their jackets and stomping on the mat.

"Where are you, darlin'?" one of them called.

"We're in here, Zach," Dusty said. "I brought company for dinner."

"So did I," the man said.

"Annie, this is my husband, Zach." Dusty leaned forward to brush her lips across his mouth. "This is the new vet in town, Dr. Annie DeSimone."

Annie couldn't help staring. Dusty's husband had male model looks, but two different colored eyes. One dark brown, one light blue, like Sean's. Broad shoulders, lean hips, muscular build. If this is what the McCray men looked like...

"Nice to meet you." Zach held out his hand and Annie shook it politely. "Oh, there you are." He turned his head as another man walked in.

"Sorry, had to stop in the kitchen to wash my hands and face," the man said.

"This is my brother Dallas," Zach said. "Dallas, meet Dr. DeSimone."

Annie looked up into the face of the most amazing man she had ever seen. Beautiful. Rugged. Dashing. He resembled Zach, but in a less refined way. He was a little taller, at least six-feet-three. His brown eyes were the color of strong coffee, and his face was perfectly shaped, except for a slight crook in his nose where it must have been broken once. The slight flaw in otherwise perfect features was not only endearing, it was sexy as hell. Unlike Zach's closely trimmed goatee, Dallas had several days' growth of beard covering his chiseled jawline, surrounding full pink lips, which were parted slightly. Annie warmed and tried not to wonder what they might feel like brushing against her own.

Moisture at the hairline rimmed his wavy black locks, forcing it into unruly curls that just touched his collar. Streaks of silver highlights graced his temples. Annie's skin tightened. Since when was gray hair sexy?

Since right now.

"Nice to meet you, Doc," Dallas said, holding out his hand.

"It's Annie," she said.

His skin was warm as his fingers tightened around hers. Big, strong hands. Capable hands. Annie loved hands. If a man didn't have good hands, she wasn't interested.

Dallas McCray had great hands.

"That's a unique accent," Dallas said. "Where are you from?"

"New Jersey." Her voice cracked, and she cleared her throat. "Outside Atlantic City."

"Yeah? What brings you here?" Zach asked.

"Just a change of scenery," Annie said, hoping they wouldn't press the issue. She wasn't ready to talk about it yet. She turned to Dusty. "I think I'll take that wine now."

"Sure." Dusty moved toward the oak bar in the corner of the room. "What do you two want?" she asked Zach and Dallas.

"Like you have to ask, darlin'," Zach said.

"Wild Turkey, I know." Dusty smiled at her husband. "What about you, Dallas? No, don't tell me. Macallan neat."

"You're a woman after my own heart, Dusty," Dallas said, winking.

The fine hair on Annie's arms straightened. Silly. Why should Dallas's words bother her? Or his harmless wink? She had just met the man.

She took the wine Dusty handed her. *Cheers,* she said to herself, and tipped the glass to her lips. Chianti. A *good* Chianti. Although she couldn't afford the good stuff, Annie knew her Italian wine. Her mother had taught her well.

"Where's the critter?" Dallas asked.

"Mona took him upstairs to settle down before dinner," Dusty said. "He's exhausted. I dragged him on my errands all day, and then, when we finally got back here, we had to go back into town with Nigel. That's how Annie and I met." Dusty explained the cat's constipation, and soon they were all in hysterics.

"Do you see a lot of constipated cats, Doc?" Dallas asked.

"Can't say that I do," Annie replied, shifting her gaze from the adorable crinkling of Dallas's eyes. "I told Dusty to keep him outside as much as possible the next few days. Trust me, you don't want to be cleaning up after him."

"Sounds like good advice," Dallas said quietly.

Annie looked up and found his gaze locked onto her breasts. She squirmed and drained her glass of wine.

"Dinner's ready, Miss Dusty."

Annie looked up to see a rotund older woman standing in the doorway.

"Thank you, Seraphina," Dusty said. "We'll be right in."

She grabbed Annie's arm. "You're going to love Seraphina's cooking."

"I'm looking forward to it," Annie said truthfully. Eating would give her something to do with her hands, which were still shaking and clammy from touching Dallas. She followed Dusty to the dining room and hoped she could get through the meal without any meatballs falling into her lap.

CHAPTER TWO

She was nothing like Chelsea.

Point one in her favor.

She was nothing like Dusty.

Point one against her.

When he filed for divorce, Dallas had decided if he ever got serious with a woman again, she would have to be a fresh-faced country girl like his sister-in-law. Someone who would devote herself to him and their family. A sweet pretty thing who didn't have a deceptive bone in her body.

Annie DeSimone was clearly a career woman. A career woman with a biting Jersey accent, no less.

So why couldn't he stop imagining her naked?

Her skin was pale and luminous, the color of moonlight. Her nearly black hair cascaded midway down her back in wavy ringlets, shining with glints of reddish burgundy that couldn't possibly be natural. Her perfect oval face blushed a creamy rose, and her beautifully formed lips held a natural pucker. And her body...even in her Bohemian skirt and loose peasant blouse, with bracelets rattling everywhere and three piercings in one ear, he could tell her curves were worth exploring.

Still, he had been with his share of beautiful women. What was it about this one?

He nodded his head to himself. It was her eyes. He had never seen anything like them before. Not blue exactly—they were almost violet. Deep amethyst. Like Elizabeth Taylor's,

TEX。

only more so. Darker and more alluring. Long ebony lashes adorned them, and the left was slightly smaller than the other, making it squint slightly when she smiled. Adorable.

He could drown in those eyes.

Of course, there was also the jolt of electricity he'd felt when their hands touched. Had she felt it too?

Probably not, he decided, as he watched her talk amiably with Dusty. When Seraphina came in to dish up seconds, Annie gushed about the sauce.

"It's wonderful," she said. "A lot like my ma's, but not quite. My ma uses caraway, but I'm thinking you use anise. Am I right?"

"Yes, my mother swore by anise," Seraphina said. "But she also used caraway from time to time."

"Have you combined the two?"

"Never have, but I've always thought about it."

"Let's do it sometime," Annie said. "We could experiment together." She took another bite of meatball, swallowed, and continued. "Your meatballs are amazing, too. Beef?"

"One hundred percent McCray raised Colorado beef," Seraphina said, laughing.

"The best in the nation," Zach piped in.

"My ma used half-beef, half-veal," Annie said, "until Pop's triglycerides went up. Then she switched to half-buffalo, half-veal, since buffalo's lower in fat. Sometimes, for a treat, she uses lamb."

"Ah, I've never tried that," Seraphina said. "It sounds good."

"It is. You need to alter the spices a little though. Less basil and more rosemary. Sometimes she uses a little fresh mint too, if she's in the mood." Annie took a sip of her wine and

Dallas tried not to stare at her mouth. "When's your next day off?" she continued. "I'd love to get together and experiment a little."

"I have Wednesdays and Sundays off," Seraphina said.

"You can experiment here anytime though, Annie," Dusty said. "Zach and I would love to feast on your results."

"Really? I'd like that." Annie wiped her lips with her napkin. "I love to cook. I haven't done anything since I got here except eat Lean Cuisines. I've been so busy getting settled and taking care of animals."

"We've got a lot of those around here." Zach smiled warmly. "And we haven't had a full-time vet in several months. Dusty's been filling in some."

"I can tell she knows a lot about animals," Annie said.

The conversation continued and Dallas listened with only one ear, hearing about every third word while he imagined Annie's plump breasts spilling out of her creamy pleasant blouse. Moonlight skin surrounding carnelian nipples. He stiffened inside his jeans.

"Dallas?"

He jerked, hearing his name. "Yeah, Zach?"

"Would you mind?"

"Huh? Would I mind what?"

"Taking Annie home. Her car's in the shop. She rode out here with Dusty."

"R-Really," Annie stammered, "it's not necessary."

"It's not a problem. I have to drive home anyway."

"But don't you live...around here?" Annie gazed around the table, all three of them chuckling. "What's so funny?"

"Nothing," Dusty said. "There's no reason you should know, being new in town. McCray Landing is the largest beef ranch in Colorado. Dallas lives here, but his home is several miles away from ours."

"Oh."

Annie's pale skin flushed, and Dallas's groin tightened. Again. He wondered if her breasts were blushing right now. Rosy swells of edible flesh.

"I knew this was the largest ranch, I just didn't—"

"Grasp the magnitude?" Dusty smiled. "I didn't either when I first came here. It's huge."

"I'll be glad to drive you home, Doc," Dallas said. "For one small favor in return."

"Wh-What would that be?"

God, her stammer is adorable. She felt the connection. He could tell.

"You let me know when you and Seraphina do your experimenting. I want to come to dinner."

Annie nodded. "Sure. No problem."

"Let's have coffee in the family room," Dusty said. "I think Seraphina made chocolate cake, too."

"No tiramisu?" Zach said.

"Not tonight, sweetheart," Dusty said. "Tiramisu is Zach's favorite dessert," Dusty explained and then followed her husband into the family room.

"I bet you make a killer tiramisu, Doc," Dallas said, helping Annie from her chair.

"As a matter of fact—"

"Yeah?"

"I can't stand the stuff."

Dallas erupted into gales of laughter. This woman was full of surprises.

"What's so funny?"

"I thought you were a good little Italian girl."

"I'm a Jersey girl, Cowboy, and don't you forget it." She broke away from his grasp and headed toward the family room.

She walked away, her narrow hips swaying gently in her voluminous skirt. With just a little urging, that frothy fabric would slide over her beautifully curved bottom and pool onto the floor, revealing legs that he was sure would be long, slender, and shapely. And between them, a moist and sweet center. He wanted a taste of her. Of *all* of her.

Damn. He needed to get laid. There hadn't been anyone since Chelsea, and those last few years their sexual encounters had been few and far between. Nothing since their separation either. Dallas's personal code of ethics wouldn't allow him to cheat on his wife.

But as of this afternoon, he no longer had a wife.

★ ★ ★

Driving home next to Dallas McCray heightened every nerve in Annie's body. Each time he shifted his five-speed Mercedes, his elbow brushed hers, and a spark ignited at the contact and ran up her arm, radiating throughout the rest of her body. This was ridiculous. He wasn't even her type.

But how could Dallas McCray not be anyone's type?

He was a cowboy, for one, and she had never had a thing for cowboys. Of course, growing up in New Jersey, she hadn't seen a lot of cowboys. Gamblers? Yes. Drunks? Yes. Hit men? A few. But no cowboys.

But a cowboy he was, and a remarkable specimen of the breed. His green western shirt was open at the collar, and a few black chest hairs peeked out. His sleeves were rolled up to his elbows and his forearms, dusted with more black hair, flexed with each shift. All that muscle and sinew. What would they feel like around her?

Then there were his hands. Big and strong. And beautiful. The man had beautiful hands.

"So you're staying in the apartment above the vet clinic?" he said.

She cleared her throat, giving herself time to answer without stuttering. "For now, anyway. I didn't bring a lot of stuff from Jersey so I don't need a lot of space."

"Is this a permanent move for you?" His voice was low and husky. Very sexy.

"I'm not quite sure yet. But I like it here so far. I'm from a big glitzy town, so this is a nice change."

Dallas chuckled softly. "Bakersville's a lot of things, but glitzy it ain't." He pulled his car into the alley behind the clinic. "I'll walk you up."

"There's no need," Annie said. If she didn't get away from him soon she feared she might throw herself into his sinewy arms.

"Doc, there's something you need to learn about us cowboys." His western drawl crept up her neck and into her ears. "We're gentlemen, and we always see a lady to her door."

"That's silly. This isn't a...date or anything."

"Doesn't make a difference, Doc." He stepped out of the car and came around and opened the door for her before she could object further. "Come on. I'll see you up."

They walked in the back door of the clinic and climbed the stairs to the entrance to Annie's apartment.

"Th-Thank you for the ride home," she said, fidgeting

with her purse.

"Aren't you going to ask me in? To thank me properly?"

"Thank you properly?" Her heart lurched. Surely he couldn't be thinking...

"Yeah. Coffee or a nightcap?"

"Oh." Heat crept up her neck. "I'm already thanking you by letting you eat dinner when Seraphina and I do our cooking together."

"All right, Doc," he said, his voice terse. "I get the picture."

Geez, now he thinks I don't like him. "I'm teasing," she said quickly. "Of course you can come in. I'm afraid I don't have coffee though. I can make a pot of tea. Well, herb tea."

"Herb tea, huh?" His drawl curved into a lazy half smile.

"Don't tell me. You hate herb tea."

"Probably as much as you hate tiramisu."

"That much, huh?" Annie forced out a laugh. "I haven't been to the liquor store yet, so I'm afraid I don't have anything else to offer you."

"Sure you do."

"Yeah? What might that be?"

"Something sweet," he said, "like this." He lowered his head and brushed his lips lightly against hers.

Annie's knees buckled at the innocent kiss. His mouth had barely touched hers, and she could hardly stand.

Dallas's strong arms snaked around her waist and pulled her close, smashing her breasts against his hard chest. "Let's try that again, Doc." He leaned down to take her lips once more.

Still gentle, he slanted his mouth over hers, outlining her lips with his tongue, nibbling across the upper then the lower. It was the most natural thing in the world to part her lips and urge him inside.

No more gentleness. His tongue swept into her mouth with carnal passion. He licked her teeth, her gums, the inside of her cheeks, the roof of her mouth.

Had she ever tasted anything quite so delicious? Chocolate. Cinnamon and cloves. And him. Dallas. *God, he can kiss.*

He tore from her mouth and settled next to her ear, nipping the soft skin just below her lobe. "Come on, Doc," he whispered, "you can do better than that."

"What?"

"Kiss me," he said. "Kiss me like you mean it." His mouth took hers again.

Like she meant it? *Damn it, why am I holding back?* She was attracted to this man. She loved to kiss. She was good at it, too. She leaned back a little, breaking his hold on her, caught his luscious lower lip between her teeth, and tugged.

Dallas groaned and pulled her tighter against him. She licked his lips, traced their sweet fullness, and then she thrust her tongue into his warmth.

If heaven were a kiss, this would be it, she thought, and then could no longer think. She only felt. And responded. Their tongues tangled together as she wrapped her arms around his neck, lacing her fingers through his silky hair. He cupped her cheeks and caressed her with his thumbs as he ravished her mouth.

They both gasped and panted, kissing each other as though the world were ending.

When they finally broke apart for a much-needed breath, Dallas trailed butterfly kisses down her cheek to her neck.

"Oh, Cowboy." Annie's voice was a breathless rasp. "You

sure know how to kiss."

Dallas nibbled his way to her ear. "So do you, Doc, when you put your mind to it." He chuckled. "I think I'll take that herb tea now."

"To hell with herb tea." Annie pushed the door open, pulled him inside, and attacked his mouth again.

"I couldn't wait to have a taste of you," Dallas said against her mouth. "All through dinner I watched you, thinking how sweet you would be."

Annie let out a soft chortle. "You were looking at my chest, Cowboy."

"And I'd love a taste of those, too."

"If you're lucky." Had she really just said that? What in God's name was she doing, seducing a man she barely knew? But she couldn't find it in herself to stop.

He cupped her breasts in his beautiful masculine hands. "What're you hiding under that pretty blouse, Doc?"

"Wouldn't you like to know?"

"Oh, yeah." He thumbed her nipples through the gauzy material, lowered his head, and bit one, right through the layers of fabric.

The wave of pleasure was so intense that Annie jerked backward.

"I'm sorry. Did I scare you?" Dallas's eyes were dark and blazing.

"No. It just... It felt really good. It's been a long time, is all."

"For me too, Doc." He touched her cheek, caressing it lightly. "If you want me to stop, tell me now."

"I... I don't want you to stop."

"Thank God." His mouth came down on hers again.

CHAPTER THREE

Frantic and impassioned, they tore at each other's clothes. Dallas ripped the filmy material of Annie's blouse right down the middle. "I'm sorry," he rasped.

"Who cares?" she said. "Just hurry."

He lifted her bra and let her breasts fall gently against her chest.

"Oh my God." He buried his face between them. He kissed the soft plump skin and then stepped back and stared. "You're beautiful, Doc. More than I even imagined." He cupped her breasts and ran his thumbs in circles around her nipples. "Dark plum nipples," he said. "I've never seen lovelier."

"P-Plum?"

"Beautiful," he said again, "I had imagined them red, but they're like your eyes, only darker. Brown. Violet. Fleshy." He lowered his head to taste one.

The searing heat of his tongue scorched her and sent blazes of fire rippling across her skin, through her body. He kissed her nipple gently at first and then sucked it between his teeth and tugged. The burn sizzled straight to her core.

"Oh, Cowboy," she said, begging, "please."

"Please what, Doc?"

"The other one." She might die an untimely death if he didn't pay attention to her other nipple. "No, take your shirt off first."

"You need to make up your mind, gorgeous." He smiled at

her, his eyes dark with desire.

"Just do it all." She tugged his shirt out of his jeans. She started unbuttoning it but got impatient and lifted it over his head. He dispensed with the offending garment and pulled her close, his chest hair tickling her already overly sensitive nipples.

"God you feel good," he said.

"Ah, yes." She pulled back. "I want to look at you."

His lips curved up in a lopsided grin. "Look all you want."

Annie lowered her gaze and drank him in. The planes of his hard chest, the sprinkling of coarse hair, his dark, fleshy nipples. He was beautifully made. "You're gorgeous, Cowboy."

"So are you, Doc."

"Kiss me again."

His mouth ravished hers with renewed intensity. She dived into the kiss, offering him even more of herself as she ran her seeking hands across his hard chest, lacing her fingers through the black curls. She fingered his nipples and relished the instant hardness her touch evoked.

When they broke the kiss for a breath, she leaned down and licked one of his brown nipples. He groaned and jerked backward.

"Damn, that feels good," he said.

"I've always wondered..." Annie's voice was low and husky. "Does breast stimulation feel as good to a man as it does to a woman?"

"I don't know," Dallas said breathlessly. "That feels pretty damn good to me, Doc." He took her plump breasts in his hands and stimulated her nipples. "Yours are very responsive though. Not all women's are."

"I suppose you've been with a lot of women, huh,

Cowboy?"

Annie closed her eyes and let the sensation of his rough fingers on her breasts take her to new heights.

"Not as many as you might think," he said, and he replaced his fingers on one nipple with his mouth.

"Ah," Annie groaned. "That's so good, Cowboy. So good." She grasped his unoccupied hand and guided it under the waistband of her skirt.

"Oh, yeah," he said, when he found her heat. "So wet, Doc. So wet for me." He glided her skirt gently over her hips until it pooled on the floor in a heap. The warmth of his fingers traveled down her flesh and stopped, tracing the small tattoo of a rose above her bikini panty line. "What's this?"

"A tattoo. What did you think it was?"

"I've never been with a woman who had a tattoo."

"Yeah?"

"Yeah. It's...pretty. It's hot."

"Glad you like it. But"—she guided his hand back inside her panties—"I think you'll like this better."

"God," he said, caressing her. He slid one finger inside her heat.

She tensed, startled.

"Sorry." He began to withdraw.

She stopped him. "No. Don't be sorry. It feels good. So good. It's just been so long..." She closed her eyes and gave herself to the pleasure. She moved her hips in rhythm with his finger, her pulse racing with the fever he generated in her.

"Take off your jeans, Cowboy."

"Yes, ma'am."

"But can you do it without moving either of your hands?"

Dallas chuckled, his breath teasing her flesh. "'Fraid not,

honey."

"I'll suffer then. But hurry."

She groaned at the loss as he removed his hands from her, pulled his boots and socks off, and fingered his belt buckle.

"Wait," Annie said. "I want to do it."

"Yes'm."

His eyes twinkled as she shoved his hands away and took over the task. Her hands shaking, she unclasped his belt and unsnapped his jeans. The zing of his zipper echoed in her ears as she slowly unwrapped her package. His hardness swelled even larger under her seeking hands. In one swoop, she brushed his jeans and boxers over his hips.

"Oh God," she said, as her mouth dropped into an oval. "You're beautiful, Cowboy."

"No one's ever said that to me before." He shuddered as she stroked his length.

"Then no one's taken the time to look." She flicked her tongue over his head and licked away a drop of liquid that had emerged. Salty. Delicious.

"You have me at a disadvantage here, Doc."

Annie grinned. "I kind of like it that way."

"Well, then, I can't complain." He stepped out of his jeans and boxers and sat down on her couch. "Do with me what you will."

"Oh no, Cowboy." She reached for his length and pulled him to his feet. "Not here. What I have planned for you requires a nice soft bed."

"Lead the way." He chuckled.

God, his voice is sexy. Low and feral with a western twang.

"I'm at your mercy."

★ ★ ★

As Annie led him by his cock into her bedroom, Dallas couldn't remember the last time he had been this turned on. When he was a teen, maybe, but that had been purely physical. What he felt right now was, well, physical, yeah, but it was also something more. He liked this woman—this beautiful, strange Jersey girl who kissed like an enchantress and had the most beautiful breasts he'd ever seen.

Maybe a woman like Dusty wasn't his future after all.

Of course, they had just met. Likely she was thinking only about sex. Yeah, sex was good. He could live with that.

"Cowboy?" Her voice trembled a little, like she was nervous. "I just want you to know." Her back thudded softly against a closed door, which he assumed led to her bedroom. "I don't sleep around."

"I didn't think you did."

"I mean, we just met and all."

"It's okay. I don't sleep around either. In fact, I'm just coming out of a nasty divorce and—" He stopped. He didn't want to think about Chelsea now.

"You're divorced? So am I. And mine was on the nasty side as well." She lowered her gaze.

"Kids?"

"No. You?"

"No."

Annie laughed, but she sounded agitated. She caught her bottom lip in her teeth. "Sorry, Cowboy. Didn't mean to kill the mood."

He took her hand and led it to his cock. "I'd say I'm still in the mood." He covered her hand with his own and smoothed it over his hardness. "How about you?"

"Yeah, I'm in the mood. You're beautiful, Cowboy. A woman would have to be dead not to be in the mood around you."

Dallas's heart lurched in his chest. He was going to bed her. This amazing, beautiful, smart woman. "Well then..."

"But..."

"Aw Geez, Doc."

"I don't want to hop into bed just because I'm feeling needy. I want it to be special."

"It'll be special."

"You know what I mean."

He gritted his teeth. Damn. "All right. I'll go."

"I don't want you to go."

Dallas inhaled sharply and let out a slow, even breath. What the hell was she after? "You're talking out of both sides of your mouth, Doc."

"I don't want to sleep alone tonight, Cowboy."

"I'll be happy to stay."

"Would you? Would you just...hold me?"

Slam. Woody killer.

"You're serious? You want me to share your bed and not make love to you? I'm not made of steel, Doc."

"I know it's selfish..."

"Selfish isn't exactly what I'd call it. I understand if you don't want to be alone, Doc, but you've got me so turned on I can hardly move. You said you had plans for me. You led me to your bedroom by my dick. What the hell was I supposed to think?"

Her cheeks flushed, and he couldn't help himself. He dropped his gaze to her incredible breasts. He had been right at dinner. They were blushing too. *Damn, she is gorgeous.*

"I'm sorry. It's just that we started talking about divorce, and when I think about my ex, it's hard for me to want to...you know. I don't want to sleep with you when he's even slightly in my mind. It would...taint it, somehow."

"Oh, Doc..."

"But I don't want to leave you hanging, either. I'm not a tease, Cowboy. I want you. I do want to sleep with you. Just not tonight. But I want you to stay."

"You're killing me."

"What if—" She smiled at him, her left eye squinting in that adorable way. "What if I took care of you?"

His woody was back. "That'd make me a pretty selfish bastard."

"No, really. I'd enjoy it, Dallas."

"That's the first time you've called me by my name." And he kind of liked it. Although Cowboy in her Jersey accent was pretty cute.

"I wanted you to know I was serious."

He thought for a moment. She really didn't want to be alone, that was apparent. He couldn't leave her. While the reason wasn't clear, she needed him, and he was a sucker for a woman in need. He wanted to stay. God only knew why, but he wanted to sleep with his arms around her. He wanted to wake up next to her and bring her coffee. Or herb tea.

"I'll stay," he said, "and you don't have to do anything."

"But I want to." Her violet gaze seared into his. "I really want to, Cowboy." She stroked him slowly, seductively. "I've never seen a more beautiful cock. As soon as I saw it I couldn't wait to get it in my mouth."

Tiny sparks ignited across his skin, and his breath caught

in his throat. "Annie, I'm trying to be a gentleman here, but you're making it damn near impossible."

"Good."

She dropped to her knees and he burst into flames.

CHAPTER FOUR

Three hundred days of sunshine a year.

Annie smiled into her pillow as morning light from her bedroom window veiled her shoulders and back. The sunshine was reason enough for her to have fallen in love with Colorado in less than a week.

There was also the handsome man next to her, whose strong arms had held her, who had whispered sweet words in her ear until she had fallen into the deepest sleep she could remember in years. She sighed, content, and stretched her arms above her head to get the blood moving.

She closed her eyes and reached toward the middle of the bed to touch Dallas's hard body. To her dismay, she patted only rumpled sheets.

He was gone.

Disappointment thudded through her body.

What had she expected? She had all but thrown herself in front of the door to get him to stay with her. Who could blame him for taking the easy way out this morning? He had probably run faster than a jackrabbit away from the sight of her. Who could blame him?

Damn him. Damn Logan Riggs for creeping into her mind when she had been about to make love with the most spectacular man on the planet.

And damn herself for being such a needy, clingy basket case. She should have let him go. Then maybe they could have started a relationship based on something other than sex, other than her codependent neediness. God, she was pathetic.

She rolled over and checked her clock. 7:10. On a Saturday morning. Boy, he sure couldn't wait to escape, could he?

Cursing herself, Annie rose from the bed and padded into her bathroom. She washed her face and hands and brushed out her unruly curls, arranging them in a high ponytail. She threw her bikinis into the hamper and pulled on a pair of sweat pants and a tank top. Her reflection in the mirror startled her. Her nipples, still dark and swollen from Dallas's attention, were completely visible through the thin white cotton. Not that it mattered. She wasn't going anywhere.

She puttered around the kitchen for a while, wondering what to have for breakfast. Cereal? Blah. Taylor ham and eggs? Too much effort. Toast and jelly? The toast would scrape the roof of her mouth. She hated that. Hell, she wasn't hungry anyway.

"Hey, Doc." A soft knock echoed, and then her door opened. He was back.

"Good, you're up," Dallas said, walking into the kitchen and looking tousled and sexy. Better than anyone had a right to first thing in the morning. He carried a cup holder holding two coffee cups.

"You're back."

"Sure I am. Where'd you think I'd go?"

"I...didn't know. I just figured you left."

"Without telling you? That wouldn't be very gentlemanly would it?"

"Er..."

"I needed some coffee, and I knew you didn't have any." He set the cup holder on the counter and took a sip from one of the cups. "I brought you something too." He smiled his lazy smile. "Herb tea. Rena's special morning blend."

As he handed the cup to her, his gaze dropped to her chest. "Wow. You do amazing things for a tank top, Doc."

Her cheeks warmed, and her nipples tightened under his gaze. She heard him take in a sharp breath. Quickly she cleared her throat.

"Who's Rena?"

"She runs the coffee shop on Main. Haven't you been there yet?"

"I haven't been anywhere, Cowboy, except on vet calls and to your brother's house."

"Tough week, huh?"

"Just busy." She took a sip from her cup. "Mmm. This is nice. What's in it? I taste mint."

"Don't ask me. Something called red tea, that's all I know."

"Rooibos."

"What?"

"Rooibos. That's red tea, though it's not actually tea. There's no caffeine in it."

"Give me coffee any day. Got to have my caffeine."

"I've nothing against caffeine, Cowboy. I just don't like the taste of coffee. That's the main reason why I don't like tiramisu. Coffee's bad enough by itself. Mix it with mascarpone, and it's disgusting. Add soggy liquor-soaked cookies, and you've got something completely inedible."

Dallas chuckled, his eyes crinkling. "I may have to rethink my stance on tiramisu, Doc. You make it sound pretty bad."

"It's the worst."

"I tried to get something for breakfast, but Rena was out

of scones, and the line for takeout at Murphy's was out the door. That's Saturday morning in Bakersville for you."

"At seven ten?"

"We're a ranching town. Everybody's up with the sun or before. Sorry about breakfast."

"No worries. I'll make you breakfast, Cowboy. What sounds good?"

He grinned at her. "Surprise me."

"Okay."

Annie took a couple of hard rolls out of her breadbox and sliced them in two. She grabbed two skillets and placed them on the stove, cracking several eggs into one. In the other, she laid slices of Taylor ham, a Jersey delicacy. Her cowboy was going to get a traditional Jersey breakfast.

She sliced some cheddar cheese while the eggs and ham were frying.

"Whatever it is, it smells good," Dallas said from his seat at her small table.

"You'll love it."

She placed two eggs, a slice of ham, and a slice of cheddar on each hard roll, set them on plates, and brought them to the table.

"Dig in, Cowboy."

He took a bite and chewed. And chewed. When he finally swallowed, Annie was laughing at him.

"It's a Jersey hard roll. Takes some effort, but there's nothing like it."

He smiled at her. God, he was so gorgeous. "The bread's delicious, but what I really like is the meat. I've never tasted anything like it. It's...tangy."

"It's Taylor ham. Taylor pork roll, actually. It's a staple

where I come from."

"I've never heard of it."

"I was surprised to find out that it's not readily available outside of Jersey. I'm glad I brought some with me, and my mother has promised to send it to me as needed."

"Who knew a Jersey girl had such secrets?"

"Oh, I've got plenty, Cowboy."

"Indeed?" He eyed her seductively.

"Oh, yeah." She twisted her lips into a smirk. "Just wait until I introduce you to Tastykakes."

"You little siren. If I wasn't enjoying this breakfast so much, I'd make you pay for that."

"Hmm. Breakfast or me? Such a hard choice. Maybe I'd better become a lousy cook if I expect to get any attention from you."

"Don't you dare. Good cooking is the way to a man's heart. Don't you know that?" He put his sandwich down and scooted his chair out from the table. "Come here, Doc."

She walked over and he pulled her onto his lap. "Dallas?"

"Yeah?"

"Thank you for...last night."

"My pleasure."

"Really. It meant a lot to me. I'm not usually so pathetically needy."

"It meant something to me, too, Doc." He grinned. "And not just because of the fantastic time you showed me in the hallway."

"That's kind of you to say."

"I'm not being kind. I'm being truthful. I like you. And you were right. If we're both coming out of divorces we shouldn't rush this."

"Mmm hmm." Annie dipped her head and pressed her lips to Dallas's neck. Musky, spicy man. "God, you smell good, Cowboy."

"On the other hand," Dallas said, as Annie felt him harden under her bottom, "maybe rushing is okay."

"Maybe," Annie agreed, running her tongue along a vein in his neck and nuzzling his pulse point. She shuddered when he cupped her breasts and thumbed her nipples.

"I can't get enough of these," he said. "You're so beautiful." He pulled her tank top up and captured a tender bud between his teeth. "Honey nipples," he whispered against her flesh. "So sweet."

The now familiar blazing tingle crept along Annie's skin as Dallas sucked her nipple. She pulled her tank top over her head, threw it to the floor, and went to work on his shirt, unbuttoning frantically and parting the fabric. She smoothed her fingers over the hard expanse of his chest as he continued to tease her nipples. She hated to stop him, but she needed that sensational mouth on hers. She grasped his head in her hands and pulled him upward, pressing their lips together. Dallas stood up, and Annie locked her legs around his hips. He walked toward the bedroom.

The phone rang.

Annie tore herself from the lip lock. "Damn."

"Ignore it," Dallas said, nibbling her neck.

"I can't. It might a sick animal."

"Doc..."

"I'm sorry, Cowboy." She unhooked her legs and picked up the phone. "This is Annie," she said.

"Hi. You're the vet, right?"

"Yeah. What can I do for you?"

"It's my horse. She's real sick."

"Okay, I'll be right there. What's your name and where are you?"

"I'm sorry. It's Catie. Caitlyn Bay. We're at the ranch adjacent to the McCrays."

"All right. Give me half an hour."

"Thank you, Doctor."

"Not a problem." She hung up, turning to Dallas. "Sick horse at the Bay ranch."

Dallas was in the process of buttoning his shirt. Annie looked guiltily at the ridge still swollen below his belt.

"I'll drive you," he said.

She smiled at him and tried to convey her sorrow at not being able to continue their tryst. "You don't have to."

"Oh? Is your car ready?"

"Crap. I forgot about that."

Dallas smiled. "It's okay, Doc. I don't mind."

Annie reached for her purse on the couch and looked around the room for her vet bag. "You're the best, Cowboy."

"Yeah. Remember that." He eyed her provocatively and her nipples tightened once again. "Doc?"

"Huh?"

"You may want to put a shirt on before we go."

★ ★ ★

The chestnut Morgan mare whinnied as Annie palpated her abdomen. Beside her stood Catie Bay, a pretty teenage girl with brown braids hanging below a creamy white Stetson. Her older brother Harper soothed the horse while Annie performed her exam. Dusty was also there, and a tall brown-haired young man with the signature McCray good looks—Dallas and Zach's younger brother, Chad.

"I called Dusty first," Catie was explaining, "and Chad was over there for breakfast so he brought her over. They both know a lot about animals, and I didn't want to bother you if I didn't have to."

"It's no bother," Annie said, running her hands over the horse's soft flanks. "That's what I'm here for."

"But it's so early. And on a Saturday."

"Not a problem. Really."

"What're you doing here, anyway?" Annie heard Chad ask Dallas.

"I brought Annie. Her car's in the shop."

"And you just happened to come across her this early on a Saturday morning?"

Annie heard the glint of sarcasm in Chad's voice. No doubt he was smirking.

"Zip it, will you?" Dallas said, his voice barely audible. But Annie had heard. She smiled to herself.

"Definitely colic," she said to Catie. "Her abdomen is distended but her temperature is normal and so are her heart sounds."

"But she's had colic before, and it's usually gone within a few hours." Catie's face twisted in anguish.

"You're describing basic spasmodic colic," Annie explained. "If she's been in distress for several days, it's a different type of colic." Annie gently patted the horse's soft coat. "She's very bloated, but I don't think it's obstructive colic. I think she may have an ulcer."

"An ulcer?" Catie's eyes widened.

"They're more common in racehorses, but ranch horses

are susceptible. Unfortunately, because of the colic, she hasn't been eating, so her stomach acid has built up which has made the ulcer worse. It's a vicious circle."

"That doesn't sound too good." Catie's voice caught in her throat.

"Well, it's not the best news," Annie said, "but it is treatable, and I think we've caught it early. With the symptoms you've described, I think it's definitely an ulcer."

"I'm so glad you're here, Annie," Dusty said. "I was sure it was just simple colic."

"You were right." Annie smiled. "But colic isn't a disease in itself. It's more often a symptom." She turned to Catie. "I'll give her a dose of medication now and leave a few more doses with you. It's all I have with me. Stop by my office anytime to pick up more."

"Yes, I sure will," Catie said.

"It's extremely important that you give her the medication on schedule, three times daily."

"Oh, I will. Don't worry."

"I'll keep my eye on her, Doc," Harper said.

"Harper, I'm a grown woman!" Catie's pretty face turned a bright crimson. "I'm perfectly capable of taking care of my animals."

The teenager glanced toward Chad McCray. The tall cowboy, deep in a discussion with Dallas, didn't appear to notice. Annie smiled to herself. Schoolgirl crush. Cute.

"Actually, I'd like to check on her tomorrow," Annie said, "so I'll bring her medication with me. There's no need for you to come by my office."

"That's kind of you," Catie said, her face still adorably red.

"Glad to."

"I'll take you home, Doc," Dallas said. "Come on."

"Okay. It was nice meeting you all."

"Come by the ranch anytime, Annie," Dusty said. "Zach and I would love to see you."

"Thank you. I will." She was growing fond of Dallas's sister-in-law.

In the car, Annie mentioned Catie's crush. "I think she has it bad for your brother."

"You're mistaken, Doc. Catie's seventeen at most, and Chad's a grown man."

"So? An older man is very sexy to a young girl. How old is he?"

"He's twenty-eight, the youngest of our brood."

"Yeah? How old are you, Cowboy?"

"Thirty-six, and Zach's thirty-one."

"Thirty-six, huh?"

"Yep. Am I too old for you? You don't look a day over thirty."

"I *am* thirty, you dumb cowpoke!"

"Dumb cowpoke? For guessing your age?"

"No woman wants to look her age. We all want to look younger."

"Oh." Dallas's eyes gleamed. "Did I say thirty? I meant twenty. Not a day over twenty. No wait. Eighteen. I mean twelve."

She punched him in the arm. "Stop that."

"You're gorgeous, Doc. If you were fifty, you'd still be gorgeous."

"Thanks. I think."

"So you're thirty. Divorced. From Jersey. Italian. A vet."

"That about sums me up. Just Bruno and Sylvia

DeSimone's little girl."

Dallas let out a guffaw. "Bruno? There are actually men named Bruno in the world?"

Annie scoffed. "This from a guy named Dallas?"

"Hey, it's my ma's maiden name. It's a popular name in these parts, though more so in Texas, for obvious reasons. Where'd Annie come from? Hardly a good Italian name for the daughter of a Bruno."

"It's a nickname. My real name is Annalisa."

"Annalisa." His husky voice caressed her name like a veil of creamy silk. "That's real pretty, Doc."

Suddenly shy, she nodded. "Thank you."

"Your skin is light for Italian ancestry."

"Not necessarily. My father's got the Mediterranean olive complexion, but my mother's fair like me."

"Your skin is the color of moonlight, and your cheeks like the palest pink rose."

For a moment, Annie thought she might melt into a puddle right in the passenger seat of Dallas's Benz. He pulled into the alley behind the clinic and came around to open her door.

"You don't have to—" she began.

"We've been through this. I'll see you to the door."

She nodded and let him take her hand as they walked into the clinic and up the back stairwell to her apartment. He took her key from her and opened the door.

"I've got to get back to the ranch, Doc. It doesn't run itself."

"I understand. It was nice meeting you." Geez, that sounded stupid. "I mean it was nice to... Well, it was *nice*."

"Ditto." He brushed his lips lightly over hers. "I'll call you later."

"You don't have to." *Geez, shut up Annie.*

"Don't you want me to?"

"Yeah. Sure I do."

He stared at her, his dark eyes burning two holes into her flesh. Several curly strands had escaped her ponytail and he tucked one behind her ear. "I changed my mind. I won't call you."

"You won't?"

"No. I'll pick you up. Around four. For dinner."

"That's awful early for dinner. Where do you want to go?"

His scalding gaze seared her from head to toe. "My place." He kissed her again, and then jaunted down the stairs, whistling a lively tune.

CHAPTER FIVE

Dallas's ranch house was even bigger and more ornately decorated than Dusty and Zach's. The giant living room was decorated almost completely in shades of white. Creamy plush carpeting covered the floor. Satin eggshell furniture surrounded a smooth white lacquer grand piano. Draperies fell to the floor in a milky cascade. The dark mahogany coffee and end tables provided a stark contrast.

"This is amazing, Cowboy."

"You like it?"

"It's beautiful."

"But do you *like* it?"

"Well, I suppose there are a few things I might've done differently, but it's truly a work of art."

"I hate it."

"You're kidding."

"Nope. All this white stuff hurts my eyes. This isn't a room where kids and dogs can play."

"Kids and dogs?"

"Yeah. I plan to rip it all out of here as soon as I can find the time to hire someone to get in here and do it right."

"If you hate it, why did you do it in the first place?"

"I didn't. Chelsea—she's my ex-wife—decorated it. Or should I say, she had it decorated. Paid some effeminate stick of a man an obscene amount of money to do this to my house." He shook his head. "I hated it then, and I hate it now."

"I suppose you're not really the New York penthouse type," Annie said.

"You got that right."

Annie opened her mouth to ask what had gone wrong between him and his ex-wife, but then thought better. He would no doubt ask her the same question, and she wasn't ready to answer it.

"What's on the menu, Cowboy? Are you cooking for me?"

"'Fraid not. I'm not really a cook. My housekeeper prepared us a gourmet feast though. It's in the fridge waiting for us to heat it up. I sent her home early."

"You mean we're alone."

"Just you and me, Doc."

"Well, then...do you think your housekeeper's feast will wait until tomorrow night?"

"Sure."

"Good. Tonight I'm cooking for you, Cowboy."

"Annie, I didn't invite you over here for that."

"Why'd you invite me then? To get me in the sack?"

His lazy grin lit up his face. "Well, if I told you the thought hadn't crossed my mind, you'd know I was lying."

"True."

"But that's not the only reason I invited you. I like you. We don't have to go to bed."

"Oh, we don't?"

"Not if you don't want to."

"I'm thinking that I do, but first I want to cook you dinner."

"Cooking is work, Doc. I don't want you to work tonight."

"Cooking isn't work, Cowboy. It's art."

"You just cooked me breakfast this morning."

"So?"

Dallas chuckled. "Hard to argue with that logic."

She gave him a friendly punch.

"I have no idea what kind of food is in the house, though," he said.

"I can work with just about anything. Lead me to the kitchen and we'll have a look."

"Oh!" Annie couldn't help squealing. Dallas's kitchen was the size of a small ballroom. Silvery granite countertops surrounded sharp stainless steel appliances. Oak hardwood graced the floor. "You brought me to this house and had no intention of letting me use this incredible kitchen? You'll pay for that one."

"I can't wait."

"You'll have to." Annie ran her hands over the smooth silver finish of the Viking cooktop. "I'm busy having an orgasm over this stove."

She turned to the stainless steel refrigerator and opened the freezer door. "Hmm. Beef, beef, and more beef. I'm seeing a pattern here."

"I'm a beef rancher, Doc."

"I suppose you have a larger freezer full of beef in the basement?"

"And in the garage."

"Okay. No problem. I can definitely work with beef." She opened the door to the refrigerator. "Eggs, good. Lettuce, good. Butter. Do you have any olive oil?"

"I haven't the slightest idea."

"I'm sure it's around here somewhere." Annie moved to the walk-in pantry. "Eureka," she said and handed him a bottle.

"This is olive oil?"

"Yeah, Cowboy. See the label? Olive. Oil. Extra virgin, no less. It's a monounsaturated fat, good for the heart. Very popular in Italy, where, by the way, they have a much lower incidence of heart disease."

"I'll remember that."

"You should. Beef is great, Cowboy, but it's extremely high in saturated fat. Although"—she eyed him up and down—"you don't seem to have any issues with fat."

She walked back into the pantry and squealed again. "Bittersweet chocolate. Excellent. I can make you a delicious dessert."

"Uh, Annie?"

"Yeah?"

"Get your pretty little bottom out here please."

"Just a minute." She couldn't tear herself away from the pantry. She grabbed the sugar and several cans of plum tomatoes.

"Now, Doc." He had sneaked up behind her and his breath was a hot whisper against her neck.

She shuddered, turning to face him. "What is it?"

He took the sugar from her and set it back on the shelf. "I refuse to play second fiddle to my kitchen." He clamped his lips onto hers.

Annie's body ignited as he pillaged her mouth. If there were an award for the world's best kisser, Dallas McCray would win it, hands down.

He walked backwards out of the pantry, dragging her with him, lifted her, and set her on the island in the middle of the kitchen. Even through her jeans, the sparkling granite was cool on her behind. He spread her legs and inched between them, pressing his hardness into her clothed sex. "Feel that, Doc?" he said against her mouth. "That's me wanting you. Hungering for you."

"Oh yeah, Cowboy," she whispered, running her tongue along his stubbled jawline. "God, you feel good."

"Better than my Viking stove?"

She laughed softly in his ear. "I don't know. What kind of heat can you generate?"

"I'll be happy to show you." He deftly unbuttoned her blouse, unhooked her bra, and threw them onto the kitchen floor. "I've been thinking about you all day," he rasped.

He tongued one nipple and then the other, the flicks sending chills rippling over Annie's skin.

"Oh," she moaned. "I've been thinking about you too, Cowboy. But..."

"But what?" He trailed kisses across the plump white skin of her breasts.

"Could you... Could you grab two pounds of round steak out of the freezer and stick them in the microwave to defrost?"

Dallas lifted his head and stared straight into her eyes. "Can you stop drooling over my kitchen for two minutes?"

Annie erupted in giggles. "I'm sorry. It's just so...amazing."

"Okay." He unbuttoned and unzipped her jeans. He removed her shoes, hoisted her bottom off the island and slid her jeans and panties over her ankles.

"Cold!" she exclaimed when he sat her naked rump back on the granite countertop.

"Serves you right. If you're going to cream over my kitchen I at least want you naked." He sank to his knees and spread her legs. "I want to make you come." He flicked his tongue into her folds. "You're already wet." He raised his head and grinned.

HELEN HARDT

"Is that for me or for my stove?"

"Can it be for both?" Annie giggled.

"Oh, you're going to pay for that one, Doc." He buried his face between her legs.

Annie's entire body quivered as Dallas's hot tongue lapped at her. The granite under her was no longer frigid, but blazing as she lifted her hips to meet his searing mouth. She hovered near the edge, ready to fly, until he slid two fingers inside her. She jumped off the cliff, moaning his name as she flew into rapture. He continued to stroke her, his fingers dancing inside her, until she came down.

"Again," he demanded and set to work. She grabbed his head and tunneled her fingers through his hair as he pleasured her. The scrape of his beard growth against her thighs, the silky roughness of his tongue—it was all too good. She screamed as she exploded once more.

"Dallas? Are you here?"

"Shit." Dallas pulled away from Annie, his face wet with her juices.

"Who is that?"

"It can't be."

He stood up and covered her naked body with his. "What the hell are you doing here, Chelsea?"

CHAPTER SIX

"Chelsea?" Annie whispered urgently. "Your wife?"

"*Ex*-wife," Dallas said between clenched teeth, still protecting her nudity with his large clothed body.

"Oh my God!" the woman shrieked, and a flash of light blond hair invaded Annie's vision.

"Get the hell out of here!" Dallas yelled. Then, to Annie, "I'm so sorry, Doc. Stay here, okay?"

He strolled out of the kitchen, wiping his face on his shirtsleeve.

Annie shivered on the counter as she listened to Dallas and his ex yelling at each other. How embarrassing. Not only was she naked, *he* was fully clothed. She looked like a cheap tramp.

"The ink isn't even dry on our divorce papers," Chelsea yelled, "and already you're tupping some little bimbo in my house!"

"This was never your house, Chelsea. It's mine. I paid you seven figures so I could keep it."

"Who is she?"

"None of your business."

"You couldn't wait, could you?"

"Hell, you have no idea how long I've waited, but it's none of your concern anymore. How the hell did you get in here, anyway? I changed all the locks."

"The door was open, Dallas."

"So you decided to just walk in? That's trespassing."

"What are you going to do? Call a cop?"

"Don't push me, Chelsea. I'll do worse to you than call a cop."

"Is that a threat?"

Annie had heard enough. She dressed quickly. She wasn't about to hide in the kitchen just because Dallas's ex had seen her naked. She was from Jersey for goodness' sake. It would take way more than an embarrassing moment to faze her. She took a deep breath, gathered her courage, and marched out to the entryway.

"Hello," she said.

"Hey, Doc," Dallas said, grabbing her hand. "You don't need to expose yourself to this unpleasantness. Why don't you wait for me in the kitchen? Or go out on the deck."

"Nonsense." She held out her hand to Chelsea. "I'm Annie DeSimone. Otherwise known as the bimbo Dallas is tupping." So they hadn't officially tupped yet. A mere technicality.

Chelsea's blue eyes widened and crimson flooded her pale face. Annie took a good look at the other woman. Strikingly beautiful. Dressed to kill. Had to be one of those Italian designers. She couldn't tell them apart—couldn't afford their clothes anyway—but she knew the style. Finally, Chelsea accepted Annie's outstretched hand.

"Nice to meet you."

"I was just getting ready to cook dinner for Dallas," Annie said. "Would you like to join us?"

"No, she would not," Dallas said. "Annie, just go out on the deck. Please? I'll handle this and I'll be out there as soon as I can."

"I wouldn't dream of it," Annie said.

"Christ," Dallas muttered.

"I came for some of my things," Chelsea said.

"You have everything you're entitled to. This was supposed to be a clean break, Chelsea."

"I just want a few of my knickknacks."

"Have your lawyer call my lawyer."

"For God's sake, Cowboy," Annie said. "Give her what she wants. You hate all this stuff anyway."

"You hate it?" Chelsea bit her lip.

"Yes, I hate it. I've always hated it. Take it all. Then leave. I want to get back to my date."

"I think I will go out on the deck after all," Annie said, suddenly uncomfortable. She strolled back toward the kitchen to the French doors leading outside.

The redwood deck was huge, complete with built-in gas barbecue and a sunken Jacuzzi. Farther out, a kidney-shaped pool beckoned, and blossoming fruit trees framed the grassy yard. Before Annie could explore further, a large black lab bounded toward her and nearly knocked her off her feet.

"Hey, fella." She stroked the dog's soft muzzle. "I'm Annie, and you are"—she fingered the clinking tags on the dog's collar—"Jet. Great name for a black dog." She scratched his cheeks as he wagged his tail and panted. "You're good company. Much better than inside. You want to show me around your yard?"

She walked down the redwood steps onto the soft grass, Jet at her heels. "Hey"—she spied a yellow tennis ball—"I bet you might like to play a little." She tossed the ball and Jet raced after it. It was slimy with slobber when he brought it back and dropped it into her hand. "That's a good boy," she said, stroking his ears. "Want to go again?" She tossed it farther this time.

She lost track of how many times she threw the ball. She had almost forgotten about dinner, when Dallas emerged from the house.

"Hey there," he said. "I see you've met Jet."

"He's great," Annie replied. "I love dogs."

"A vet who loves dogs?" Dallas grinned. "I can't picture it."

"Ha-ha," she said, tossing the ball once more. Then she strode over to Dallas. "Listen, Cowboy. Maybe I should take a rain check on this dinner thing."

"But you said you wanted to cook for me."

"Yeah. I do. But, I'm thinking the mood has been killed here. Make that murdered. By a vengeful blonde." She giggled nervously.

"I'm really sorry. She's gone now." He flashed his lazy half smile. "And I locked all the doors."

Annie sighed. She had wanted this evening to work out. But, "I can't compete with her, and to tell you the truth, it's not in me to try."

"Compete with her? What the hell are you talking about, Doc?"

"If that's the kind of woman, you're used to—"

"That's the kind of woman I spent lots of money getting rid of."

"Oh, come on, Cowboy. She's beluga caviar, and I'm fish and chips."

"Hey"—he stroked her cheek—"I like fish and chips."

"We hardly know each other."

"So? We can't get to know each other?"

"I suppose so, but don't you think maybe we should have a real date? I mean, we seem to have a good...chemistry together, but—"

"Chemistry? We explode, Doc. We're dynamite. The earth moves a little faster when we're in the same room together. I knew it when I first laid eyes on you."

Annie threw the saliva soaked ball again. "I don't know if I'd put it *that* way."

"How exactly would you put it?"

She sighed. He was right. "Okay, we're dynamite together. We explode." Why fight it?

"Exactly." He pulled her into his arms and brushed his mouth over hers. "Let's start over. I don't want you cooking tonight. You can cook tomorrow night."

"Tomorrow night? What if I'm busy?"

"Are you?"

"No."

"Okay then."

"Why can't I cook tonight?"

"Because I want to pamper you. Let me feed you."

What a sweet man. "All right, Cowboy." She wrapped her arms around his neck. "Feed me."

★ ★ ★

"It was horrible, Daddy." Chelsea Beaumont McCray cried into her cell phone. "He had a naked bimbo in my kitchen! And she had an accent. Jersey City or Philadelphia. They all sound alike to me. Low-class."

"Now, buttercup," Stewart Henderson Beaumont said, "he's no longer your husband. He has the right to cavort with whomever he chooses."

"I'm almost positive he was cheating on me while we were

married." Chelsea sniffed.

"He was cheating on you?" Her father's thunderous voice hurt her ear.

Chelsea knew better. Dallas would never cheat. His cowboy ethics wouldn't allow it. Cowboy ethics that got on her nerves. Oh, he was faithful to her all right, but his code of the west hadn't kept him from throwing her over. What had she done to deserve that? Well, there were a few things, but still.

Her father, however, didn't need to know about his ethics. "I don't know for sure, Daddy. But he might have. I mean, we're barely divorced and he already has a hussy in his home. He was probably fooling around with her before he even filed for divorce."

"Jason McCray's boy? I don't know, Chelsea."

Damn him anyway. Taking the fool's side. "I swear it, Daddy," she said. "Now that I think of it, I'm absolutely sure I've seen the woman before. Sneaking out of our barn!"

"You wouldn't be stretching the truth a little, now would you?"

"Come on, Daddy," she said sweetly. "You know me."

"Yes, I do know you, Chelsea. And I love you. But you've always been willing to do anything and everything to get what you want. The man gave you a fair settlement. Best cut your losses on this one, sugarplum."

Chelsea hit end, threw down her phone, and grabbed two fistfuls of her hair. Dallas had even turned her father against her. Life was not fair.

On the other hand, there was one person who might take her side. Grinning to herself, she retrieved her phone and punched in some numbers.

★ ★ ★

Stewart Beaumont sighed. He loved his daughter, but she was better off out of her marriage. Dallas McCray had actually been quite fair with her. The seven-figure settlement had set her up for life. She had plenty of money. So what was the problem?

"Still here, Stew?" Jon Parker, his chief legal officer and an old school chum of Chelsea's, poked his tousled blond head into the office.

"Just finishing up," Stewart said. "You?"

"On my way out. Want to grab a drink?"

"Yeah. I could use one. I just got off the phone with Chelsea. She has some weird idea that McCray was cheating on her before the divorce."

"Really?" Jon's cell phone started playing Mozart's sonata. "Excuse me." He pulled the cell out of his pocket. "Oh, speak of the devil." He hit send. "Hi, Chels. What's up?"

CHAPTER SEVEN

"This is the life, Cowboy." Annie took a sip of wine and set her goblet on the edge of Dallas's sunken hot tub. The luxurious frothy warm water rolled over her body, soothing her aching muscles. Her plump breasts bobbed lightly on the surface.

"I'm glad you like it," Dallas said, winking. "But what are you doing way over there?" He sat opposite her, his arms stretched out on either side of him. "Why don't you come sit with me?"

"Mmm. Sounds good, but I can't move." Annie closed her eyes and inhaled the pungent eucalyptus oil that Dallas had sprinkled into the bubbling water. "It's been a really busy week. I didn't realize how exhausted I was until I stepped into this little bit of heaven on earth."

Dallas held out his arm. "Come here. I can help you relax."

"I bet you can." Annie smiled and took his hand. Within seconds, she was on his lap, straddling him, his hardness pressing into her. "Is that a cucumber in your pocket or are you just glad to see me?"

Dallas chuckled at her bad line. "I'm *very* glad to see you." He wriggled under her, parting her and teasing her entrance. "Are you protected?" His sexy voice rasped.

"I'm on the pill," Annie said, "and it's been a long time."

"For me too. Both clean then."

He nudged his way inside and Annie groaned, the

slickness of the water around her folds adding a sensual layer to the feeling of completion as his erection stroked her. "Ah," she moaned. "So good, Cowboy."

"You fit me like a glove, Annie. So tight. So sweet."

They moved together, the warm water sloshing about them as they rode each other. Annie leaned into Dallas's hard form, sliding against him, her nipples scraping against his damp and springy chest hair. She claimed his mouth, and his groan fueled her passion. Her climax ripped into her suddenly, like a lightning strike out of a clear summer sky. She screamed his name and felt his release.

Every single pulse of it.

Sated, she slumped into him. His lips nipped at her neck and ears. "Wow, Doc."

"Yeah. Wow."

"Told you we were explosive."

"Seems you were right."

He stood up with her in his arms, the slick water dripping from them.

"What are you doing?"

"I'm taking you to my bed."

"Yeah. Bed is good. Sleep."

"I don't have any intention of sleeping."

"Oh?" She smiled against the roughness of his cheek.

"I'm going to taste every inch of your luscious body."

"Oh you are?"

"You bet your sweet little bottom, Doc."

"Well, in that case"—she flashed him what she hoped was a teasing grin—"you know what they say."

"What's that?"

"Payback's a bitch."

★ ★ ★

No one had ever paid such exquisite attention to her body. Dallas worshiped her with his hands, his mouth, his tongue, all the while murmuring to her how beautiful she was, how hot she made him. He was particularly enamored with her breasts.

"So beautiful," he said, tormenting her nipples with little licks, little tugs. "Like nothing I've ever seen before. You should have been born centuries ago. Renaissance painters would have captured you on canvas for all eternity. Poets would have written odes to you. Wars would have started over you. Your dark curls, your violet eyes, your ruby lips. Your dusky plum nipples." He traced one areola with his tongue. Her skin contracted. "You're a goddess, Annie."

Who knew words could be such a powerful aphrodisiac? Not Annie. Dallas made love to her with words as well as his body. She hissed as he drove her nipples into a frenzy with his tongue, and then released each one only to bite and nip at her plump white flesh.

"I adore you," he said. "I adore every inch of you, Doc. You're so beautiful."

He paved a trail down her belly with his mouth, tickled her navel, and traced the lines of her tattoo. When he reached her raven curls he buried his nose in them and inhaled. "Mmm," he said. "Sugar and spice."

"And everything nice?" Annie laughed, her voice shaking.

"Everything *very* nice." He lowered his head to her moist sex and inhaled again. "Sugar and spice and sweet, sexy woman." His voice was a husky growl.

She shuddered as his tongue danced across her heated

flesh. He sucked and pulled at her slick folds, making hungry and satisfied noises. Her body throbbed at each fresh attack. She grew wetter and wetter.

"Nice, Doc, nice." Dallas's words veiled her scalding sex in heated breath. "So wet for me. So sweet." He tugged at her flesh, and then sucked all of her between his lips.

"Oh!" She nearly jumped off the bed.

He lifted his head. "Too much?"

"God, no. Too good, is all."

He smiled, his lips shining with her cream. "No such thing." Then he bent back to his work.

Dallas expertly brought Annie just to the brink of climax several times, releasing her before she could find bliss. "You're killing me, Cowboy."

"Anticipation," he said, grinning. "Think about how good it will be when you finally explode."

"I'm going to explode on you if you don't let me come."

"Mmm. Tempting." He nibbled at her swollen clit. "But I think you've suffered enough." He swirled his hot tongue around the nub of flesh while he slid two fingers into her heat.

"Oh, yeah. Like that." Annie closed her eyes and arched her back as Dallas's talented hands and mouth catapulted her over the edge. She grabbed his head and ground violently into him as the rapture took her higher and higher.

When she returned to her body and opened her eyes, Dallas, still between her legs, was gazing at her.

"God, you're beautiful when you come," he said.

"I never thought about what I look like."

"Why?"

"Because it's embarrassing. You're not supposed to be watching me. You're supposed to be...you know...servicing me."

"Servicing you, huh?" He inched forward. "Does that mean you have complaints?"

"Of course not. It's just... I don't want you watching me."

"God. You're gorgeous. Why not?"

"Because I probably look like a freak, that's why. For all I know I have drool pouring out of my mouth."

"If you're drooling over me, I can handle it."

Annie punched him halfheartedly in the arm. "I just don't want you to see me lose control."

"Watching you lose control is a huge turn on, Doc." He led her hand to his erection. "See?"

"Oh." Annie caressed the smooth, hard flesh. "I love the feel of your cock. It's so warm and velvety. And hard. So fucking hard, Cowboy."

"Only for you." Dallas lowered himself and rubbed his stubbled cheek over Annie's smooth one, smearing her with her own juices. "All that wetness. All for me. I want you." He brushed his lips over hers. "Taste yourself," he said. "Taste yourself on me." He traced his tongue over her lips and thrust it inside her mouth.

Annie sighed, opening herself to the kiss. She tasted her own tanginess mingled with the spicy and robust taste of Dallas. Her lover. Her man.

God I want him to be my man.

"Take me, Cowboy," she said against his mouth. "Make love to me."

With a single hard thrust, he was inside of her. Sweet stroking. Smooth joining. Like nothing before. Annie arched to meet every plunge, urging him deeper and deeper into her body. She wanted to merge with him. Join not only their bodies but their souls. She looked into his eyes and was surprised to find them open.

"That's it, Doc. Take me in. Take all of me."

"God, yes."

"Look at me. Watch me love you."

She fixed her gaze onto his and lifted her head to look between their bodies. She quivered at the rhythmic beauty of his body joining to hers. "Oh, Cowboy. We look beautiful together."

"Yeah, Doc. My sweet Doc." His jaw clenched. "I can't last much longer. You feel so good. Like you were made for me."

Annie was near completion herself. "Don't wait. Come for me, Cowboy. I'll come when you do. I want us to come together."

One. Two. Three more thrusts, and his cock began to pulsate against her sensitive walls. Annie let go, the sparks tingling across her body and propelling outward until ecstasy claimed her. Dallas moaned her name, and she moaned his, and together they exploded in a fiery embrace.

Afterward they lay together, a tangle of arms and legs.

"That was amazing," Dallas said. He stroked her tousled curls and brought one to his nose. "Every part of you smells good. Your hair. It's like a coconut grove." He smiled. "Did you enjoy yourself?"

"Do you even have to ask?"

He laughed. "Even as a young man, a night like this would have put me out cold."

"Oh?"

"But now, I'm middle-aged, and all I can think about is making love to you again." He nudged into her with his erection. "See?" He let out a raspy chuckle. "There are still a few places on your body that I haven't tasted yet."

"Oh, my gorgeous Cowboy." Annie caressed his taut back, his firm buttocks, and her breath caught at his male beauty. "It's going to be a long, sweet night."

★ ★ ★

Dallas propped his head on his elbow and gazed at the woman in his bed. She slept soundly on her stomach, the moonlight from his window veiling her in a shimmering cloak. The sheets were rumpled at her waist. He smoothed his hand over the glowing skin of her back. She was so soft. He'd never known a softer woman.

He had made good on his promise to taste every inch of her—every inch of her was delicious, too, like a fresh peach pie—and she'd paid him back in spades. He smiled, remembering. Then he'd made love to her again. Slowly this time. A lingering and sensual coupling followed by a climax so intense he'd nearly wept with the pure joy of it.

It scared the hell out of him.

Annie DeSimone was like no one he'd ever known, certainly not the type of woman he thought he'd ever fall for. But she was beautiful, intelligent, funny. An amazing and generous lover.

He was falling hard.

He sighed and raked his fingers through his disheveled hair. Why think about that now? Why not just enjoy the moment? His night with this beautiful and unbelievable woman. He snuggled up to her warm body and fell into a deep sleep.

★ ★ ★

He awoke when the sun rose and shone through his window, the rays warming his skin. Annie's back was snuggled against his chest, spoon fashion. Jet waggled up to the bed, wanting attention. His tongue darted out to lick Annie's face.

"Go on, boy," Dallas said, waving him away. "She's mine." He brushed his lips against Annie's smooth shoulder and reached between her legs. She let out a small squeak as he stroked her, and when he slid into her, she sighed, her eyes still closed.

"Morning," he murmured and kissed the sensitive spot below her ear.

"Mmm." She wiggled her bottom and gave him better access.

"Sleep well?" he asked.

"Mmm," she said again. "Perfect."

"Me too."

Languidly he made love to her and cherished the sweet suction as her walls hugged him. He had always enjoyed sex, but since when had it felt this good? Since when had he been able make love to a woman three times and still want more? He smiled into her neck.

"You're something, Doc."

"Mmm. You too, Cowboy."

He moaned in her ear. "I can't last much longer."

"S'okay." She grabbed his hand and led it to her clit.

He stroked her until she started to convulse, and then he let himself go.

He wrapped her in his arms and snuggled into her until his heart rate returned to normal. Absently he thumbed her nipples, pinching and fondling them. Her contented sounds told him he pleased her.

"Hey, Cowboy."

"Hmm?"

"I need to get up."

"Later." He inched his fingers lower, drawing invisible circles on her taut belly, tickling her navel.

She giggled into her pillow. "I don't think there's anything I'd rather do than spend the entire day in bed with you, Cowboy, but I have a horse to check on."

"I like the first idea." Dallas pressed his lips to her neck and inched his fingers lower. "You smell like tulips in springtime."

"Cowboy?"

"Hmm?"

"What if it were *your* horse?"

"Hittin' me where it hurts. That's not fair, Doc."

"I thought that might get you." She removed his fingers from her nest of dark curls. "Oh, I do hate to get up."

"Then don't."

"I need a shower."

"What if I refuse to let you use my bathroom?"

She turned over to face him and slapped him playfully. "Then I may wet the bed, Cowboy."

"I have a full-time housekeeper." He grinned at her. "She doesn't ask questions."

"You're impossible."

"I thrive on it." He took her mouth in a scalding kiss. "I can't get enough of you," he said against her lips.

"I know the feeling." She returned the kiss with a searing one of her own. "But I really. Have. To. Get. Up." She pushed at his chest and broke his hold on her. "I'm sorry. Truly."

"Not half as sorry as I am."

She walked, naked, toward his bathroom. *Damn, she's perfectly formed.* His cock twitched again.

"Put your tongue back in your mouth," she said jovially, her back to him.

"What makes you think I'm watching you?"

"Aren't you?"

"Hell, yes." He hooted in laughter. "Any red-blooded male who wouldn't watch you any time he could is a lunatic."

"Or gay." She laughed. "Or blind. Or too old to—"

"I get the idea." He sat up and stretched, his blood bursting through his veins. He couldn't remember when he had felt so well rested. Odd, since he hadn't done much sleeping.

When he heard the whoosh of the shower, he stood up, imagining streams of water pelting down that gorgeous body. If she was going to shower, he was damn well going to shower with her.

She was massaging shampoo into her hair when he sneaked into the shower behind her. He smoothed his fingers over her shapely bottom and she jumped.

"Sorry, Doc."

"You might warn me next time. Damn, I got soap in my eye."

"I'm sorry, gorgeous." He turned her to face him. "Here. Let me."

He grabbed a washcloth, wet it, and gently rinsed out her eyes. He turned her into the water stream, rinsed her hair, and brought her back around to face him. Her hair hung in dark wet ringlets, clinging to the swell of her breasts. He lowered his lips to hers and kissed her hard.

When she encircled her arms around his neck, he knew she had surrendered. He lifted her off the ground and she wrapped her legs around his hips. He entered her with one swift thrust.

"Mmm, Cowboy," she said. "You're insatiable. You can't be thirty-six. Are you sure you're not nineteen?"

"I can't seem to get enough of you," he said through clenched teeth. "Damn. I'm sorry, Doc. I'm coming in for a landing."

"I'm right there with you." She panted and moaned his name, and every spasm of her walls clamped him in sweet tightness.

Annie lowered her legs and slowly slid down his body. She laid her cheek against his chest and twirled her tongue around a hard male nipple. His whole body trembled.

"Mmm," she said. "For a cowboy and a gentleman, you're an awesome lover, Dallas."

He knew he had a stupid grin on his face. He couldn't help it.

★ ★ ★

"Did Joe say when your car would be ready?" Dallas asked Annie over breakfast.

"No. He probably won't even get to it until tomorrow. I assume he takes the weekends off." She petted Jet's soft head and fed him a scrap of scrambled egg.

"True. Only us ranchers work the weekends around here. I'll drive you over to the Bay place this morning, and then I'll take you home."

"Thanks, Cowboy. You're a darned cute chauffeur." She loved teasing him. What was it about this man? "But I need to go home first. I promised Catie I'd take over the rest of the mare's medication."

"Not a problem."

She leaned forward and planted a kiss on his sexy mouth. "I am really glad I met you, Dallas McCray."

"Me too, Doc, and not just because of the sex."

"I don't know. The sex is pretty good," Annie said, teasing.

"Hell, yeah. But I like you, Doc. You're special."

"I like you too, Cowboy." Oh yes, she liked him. She *really* liked him. She downed the last gulp of her water. Dallas didn't have any tea or herb tea in the house, a problem he had promised to remedy before her next visit.

"You still cooking me dinner tonight?" He rose and took his plate to the sink.

"Sure. If you want me to."

"You bet."

"Then take out two pounds of round steak to defrost. I'll bring the rest." In her mind, Annie began planning an elaborate Italian menu.

"You sure? The grocery's not open on Sundays."

"Crap."

"Small town, Doc."

"I didn't think of that. Do you want a rain check?"

"Nope. You can use what I have here. You said so last night."

"Okay. That'll work," she said. "But right now, we need to get over to the Bays', and then I need to get home. I still have a lot of unpacking to do."

"Need help?"

"Not that kind of help, Cowboy. If you stay with me all day, do you really think I'll get any unpacking done? Besides, last time I checked you have a ranch to run here."

"True. Plus, the rodeo starts up in a couple weeks."

"Rodeo?"

"Yeah. It's regional. Held here for six weeks every summer. We get some pretty good cowboys, though not as many as the national stock show in Denver."

"Do you...rodeo?"

He laughed, his gorgeous eyes crinkling. "I used to, a little. Not any more though. It was never really my thing."

"What is your thing, Cowboy?"

"Shooting, I guess. I'm a crack shot."

"A cowboy who doesn't ride."

"Oh, I ride. I just don't compete. That's more Zach and Chad's thing. They still compete, and Dusty used to."

"Dusty? Sweet little Dusty?"

"Sweet little Dusty is a hell of a bull rider."

"No kidding?"

"Yeah, believe it or not. Competed as a barrel racer. Was darn good at it too, but she gave it up when she got pregnant."

"Good choice."

"We all thought so. I'll be happy to take you to the rodeo. Opening night."

"Sounds great. I've never been to one. This may surprise you, but we don't have many rodeos in Jersey." Annie giggled. Then, "Oops, I almost forgot. Could you hand me my pocketbook?" She motioned to her handbag on the counter.

"Pocketbook?"

"Yeah, there." She pointed again.

"That's a purse, Doc."

"In Jersey it's a pocketbook." She took it from him. "I need to take my pill."

"Pill?"

"Just my birth control pill. I take them in the morning. You'd think after all these years I'd remember. I'm terrible about forgetting. I keep an extra month's worth in my purse for just such an occasion. After last night, I sure don't want to be even a few hours late taking it."

"Yeah, that could be a problem." He tossed her the purse. "After all these years? So you and your husband never wanted kids?"

"Oh *he* did. I did too. Just not with him."

"Oh?"

"I decided I didn't want to get pregnant. After a while, he assumed I was infertile from—" She cleared her throat. She didn't want to get into that. "Anyway, I was always on the pill."

Dallas's lips pressed together and the muscles in his face tensed. Had she angered him?

"You all right?"

"You didn't tell your husband you were on the pill?"

"No."

"Why not?"

"I had my reasons." None of which she cared to discuss with him. Or anyone.

"I see." He stood up and fisted his hands around the back of his chair, his knuckles white with tension.

"What's wrong?"

"Let's get you to the Bays', Annie, and then home. You're right. I have tons of work to do around here."

CHAPTER EIGHT

He had promised his mother he'd come for supper. On a Sunday evening. That was the excuse Dallas gave Annie when he broke their date for her to cook him dinner. No offer to take her with him to meet his sainted mother. No offer of a rain check.

He had hardly spoken to her as he drove her to her office to get medication for Catie's horse, back to the Bay ranch, and then to her apartment. If he hadn't wanted to be with her, why hadn't he just taken her home and let her make her own way over to the Bays'? Sure, she had no car, but she had a feeling Catie or her brother would have gladly driven into town to fetch her.

Because Dallas had said he'd do it, and he wouldn't go back on his word. He was the consummate gentleman.

It was starting to get on her nerves.

She thought back on their morning. He had made love to her twice, had all but begged her to stay with him for the day, and then suddenly he had become distant.

What had they been talking about? The pill. She was on the pill, and had been on it all through her marriage to Riggs. For good reason. Why would that upset him?

He had kissed her goodbye, but it was a light brush of his lips on her cheek. Then he had cupped her face in his hands and stared into her eyes for a few seconds. He had wanted to kiss her. Thoroughly. She was sure of it. His need and desire were so thick she could feel it in the air, but he had backed away.

"I'll see you around, Annie," he had said. Not "I'll call you later." Not "When can I see you again?"

He'd called her Annie, not Doc.

He probably wanted time to think. Sure. That was it. Time. They had only just met. She could give him time. Hell, she should want time herself.

But she didn't. She wanted to be in his arms. In his bed.

She sighed and picked up the box containing her college degree and her veterinary doctorate. Time to hang them in the office downstairs. She pulled out the framed and matted diploma.

Annalisa DeSimone Riggs. Doctor of Veterinary Medicine.

She made a mental note to contact the university and get a new copy of her degree, minus the Riggs. She didn't want to think about him every time she glanced at the wall in her office.

She plunked into her office chair and raked her fingers through her curls, matted from perspiration. She inhaled. Sweaty horse. Riggs had hated how she smelled after working with animals. He'd hated so much.

Damn him. Damn Logan Riggs.

And damn Dallas McCray. Stupid cowboy. The truth cut through her heart. He didn't want time. He had just wanted sex. It had been about the sex all along, and now he was done.

Were all men truly assholes? Why couldn't she catch a break? Again, she dropped her gaze to her veterinary degree.

Annalisa DeSimone Riggs, the doctorate jeered. The print pulsed against the stark white contrast, mocking her. *You're nothing but a whore, a goddamned bitch. Only good for a fuck.*

Only good for a fuck. Clearly, Dallas saw her the same way.

She threw the framed degree against the wall, her heart thundering. As shards of glass speckled the carpet, Annie burst into tears and cried for a long time.

★ ★ ★

He didn't call.

By Thursday Annie had resigned herself to the fact that her affair with Dallas McCray had been just that—an affair. A one-night stand that had lasted for a weekend. A glorious weekend of mind-boggling sex. That was it.

She was no stranger to disappointment. She could get over this hurdle. All things considered, it was nothing. She hardly knew Dallas McCray.

So why did she feel such an acute loss, like a limb had been ripped from her body?

The vibration of her cell phone against her hip jolted her out of her barrage of self-pity. What was wrong with her anyway? She had long ago learned how to pick up the pieces of her life and move on.

"This is Annie."

"Hi there. It's Dusty McCray."

Crap. A McCray.

"Hey, how's Nigel doing?"

"All better, thanks to you."

"Glad I could help."

"Oh you did. Though it was an interesting couple of days." Dusty's voice rippled with laughter. "Anyway, I was wondering if you're free this Saturday."

"Oh?"

"Yeah. Zach and I are having a barbecue out at the ranch. My brother's coming into town. I'd love for you to meet him."

"Well..." She didn't need to ask the question. Of course Dallas would be there. He was Zach's brother. She cleared her throat. "Sorry. Frog." She hesitated again. Then, "I don't know, Dusty. I've still got a lot of unpacking to do."

Dusty's husky giggle echoed in her ear. "You work too hard, Annie. I'm going to have to insist. Around four, okay? Is your car out of the shop? If not, I can have someone pick you up."

God, no.

"I have my Bug back, but thanks."

"Too bad. I'm sure Dallas would have been glad to bring you." Dusty's tone was teasing.

"I'm not so sure."

"He chauffeured you around all last weekend, and he didn't seem to have any complaints."

"He was just being gentlemanly," Annie said, trying to think of a way to end this conversation. Quickly. "Besides, I haven't seen him since Sunday."

"Really?" Dusty's voice registered surprise. "I could have sworn you two hit it off."

"Apparently not." She rolled her eyes. She didn't want to be rude. Dusty had been her first friend in Bakersville, and she didn't want to offend her, but— "I'm sorry. I need to go."

"Okay. We'll see you at four on Saturday."

"Yeah, I'll be there. Thanks, Dusty. Bye." She had never been so glad to hit end.

Oddly, her afternoon turned out to be free. No animal emergencies, no appointments, no walk-ins. She took the time to walk around and familiarize herself with her new home town. When she walked by the auto repair shop, she waved to Joe.

"How you doin', Dr. D?" he called.

"Call me Annie. And I'm good, thanks."

"How's your Bug runnin'?"

"Great." She continued walking.

"Hey, Annie. Wait a minute." He left the car he was working on and walked toward her, rubbing his greasy hands on a red cloth.

"Yeah? What is it?"

"Where're you off to?"

"Kind of taking the afternoon off," she said. "I haven't had the chance to wander around since I got here."

"I'm due for a break. Can I buy you a coffee?"

Annie regarded the mechanic. Clad in blue coveralls and covered in black, he was still handsome, with searing blue eyes and silky chestnut hair pulled back in a low ponytail. Was he asking her out? Or was he just being friendly?

She smiled to herself. What did it matter? "Sure, Joe, that'd be fine."

"Cool." Cool? Man, he couldn't be more than twenty-two. "Give me two minutes. I'll wash up and be right with you."

Annie was admiring a vintage Corvette when Joe sidled out. She nearly jumped out of her skin when she saw him. Levis sagging at just the right spot on lean hips, broad shoulders clad in a Ralph Lauren polo. Hardly the clothes for a little town in the west. He had combed his hair and re-secured it behind his neck.

"You ready?" he asked.

"Yeah. Sure." She ran her fingers over the blue sports

car's sleekness. "Whose car is this, Joe?"

He grinned at her. His lips weren't as full and shapely as Dallas's, but they were darn nice nonetheless. "It's mine."

"No kidding?"

"Yeah. I work on her in my spare time. You wanna go for a ride?"

"Don't you have to get back to work?"

"Nah. It's a slow afternoon. And Brady's there for anyone who walks in."

"Are you sure?"

"It's called Joe's for a reason, Annie. It's my business, so I can come and go as I please. That's the way I like it."

His business. Maybe he was older than she thought. "Can I ask you a question?"

"Sure enough."

"How old are you?"

"Thirty-one."

Her eyes widened. "Wow. I'd have thought you were much younger."

"Why? How old are you? Wait. Let me guess." He eyed her up and down, his sizzling gaze heating her body. "I'd say about twenty-seven?"

Annie burst out laughing.

"Did I say something humorous?" Joe asked, his eyes confused.

"Not at all, Joe." She linked her arm through his. "You just made my day is all. I'd love that ride now."

"I'd have guessed even younger," he said, opening the passenger door of the Corvette, "but I knew you'd have to be at least twenty-five when you finished vet school."

Smart, too.

"It's only two blocks to Rena's," he said, sliding into the driver's seat next to her. "We'll have a coffee, and then I'll take you on a *real ride*."

Annie winced slightly at the double entendre. Surely he hadn't meant it that way.

"So"—she leaned forward and smoothed her fingers over the glossy leather console—"how long have you lived here in Bakersville?"

"My whole life. Grew up on a ranch, a small operation, near the McCray place. Horses and cattle were never my thing though."

"Let me guess. Cars were your thing."

"You got it. Give me chrome over cowhide any day." He laughed as he pulled in front of the coffee shop.

While Annie hated the taste of coffee, its aroma was something else altogether. The robust fragrance wafting out of the small haven intoxicated her. Before Joe could touch the door handle, it opened on its own, and Annie found herself face to face with Dallas McCray.

"Ow!" she exclaimed. Dallas had dropped his cup of coffee and the hot liquid spattered over Annie's sandaled toes.

"Christ, McCray," Joe said. He hurried inside the shop.

"I'm sorry," Dallas mumbled.

Annie sighed. "It's a good thing I didn't wear my white sandals today." She laughed nervously.

"Are you hurt?" He reached toward her, but quickly whisked his hand into his pocket, as though thinking better of touching her. "Thank God it was a mocha. The milk cooled it down. If it had been hot coffee..."

Annie glanced down at her toes, red from the heat. "I doubt it's life threatening, Dallas. Don't worry about it."

Joe returned with a damp cloth. He knelt down and wiped off Annie's feet. "Your silver toenail polish is very sexy, Annie," he said.

Annie was still watching Dallas. His forehead wrinkled at Joe's comment, and his eyes, darker than the coffee in the shop, seared into her. Annie shuddered. A few nights ago, Dallas had kissed every inch of her body, including her toes. He had liked the silver polish also. "You have incredible feet, Doc," he'd said. "You got a foot fetish, Cowboy?" she had teased him back. "Only for your hot silver toes," he'd said, and proceeded to pamper them with kisses and an incredible foot massage.

Her heart quickened at the memory.

Joe got to his feet. "All better?"

"Yeah. Thanks, Joe." She couldn't take her eyes from Dallas. Her skin was blazing from his heated gaze. She wanted to touch him. To pull him into her body. To kiss him senseless.

"Ready for a coffee?" Joe asked.

"Annie hates coffee," Dallas said.

"Oh. Why didn't you tell me?"

"I figured I'd have tea," Annie replied.

"Great. If you'll excuse us, Dallas." Joe took Annie's hand and steered her into the shop, leaving Dallas on the sidewalk, his brow furrowed and lips pursed.

"He could have apologized," Joe said, holding out a chair for Annie.

"He did. While you were getting the towel."

"Not much of a talker is he?" Joe sat down across from her. "He never was. Absolutely no sense of humor either."

No sense of humor? She and Dallas had shared an easy banter that had kept them both in stitches.

"Do you know Dallas well?" she asked.

"Not too well. I went to school with his brother Zach. He was never much of a talker either. He's loosened up though since he got married."

"I know his wife. She's very nice."

"Yeah, a pretty little thing, too. Their son's adorable."

"He is," Annie agreed.

"Dallas, though, he's an enigma. He went and married some rich east coast girl right out of law school."

"Law school?" Annie said. Clearly there was a lot she didn't know. "Dallas McCray's a lawyer?"

"Licensed, yeah. Went to Yale. But he doesn't practice, so far as I can tell. He's a rancher at heart."

"I see."

"Anyway, they're divorced now. The younger one, Chad, he's never been married." Joe let out a guffaw. "He's a lot more fun than the other two."

"How so?"

"Likes to party. Always laughing. Never serious. A love 'em and leave 'em kind of guy. He got all the personality and sense of humor, I think." Joe rose to his feet. "Tea, you said?"

"Yeah. Thanks."

"I'll be right back." He winked at her.

Joe was attractive. Funny. Smart.

But he wasn't Dallas McCray.

★ ★ ★

There was a knife in Dallas's gut.

A dull, jagged knife that tore into his flesh.

A knife named Annie DeSimone.

He wanted to kick the snot out of Joe Bradley, and for what? Buying his girl a cup of tea? Hell, she wasn't his girl. He didn't want her. Couldn't go down that road again. He would never get involved with a woman who was capable of deceiving her husband.

Still she haunted him day and night. He dreamed of her smooth skin, her sweet kisses, her lovely body.

If only things had been different.

The knife in his gut was buried deep, and he wondered if he'd ever be free again.

★ ★ ★

Fifty thousand dollars.

Morgan Bailey cleared his throat. "Okay," he said to the tall man on the bar stool next to him. He met all kinds at the Sour Mash Saloon. The hub of Lorna, a small town that made Bakersville look like a thriving metropolis, the Sour Mash attracted local ranch hands, due mostly to its dollar beers from four to six p.m. daily.

"Okay what?" The man arched his dark brows.

Morgan took a deep swallow of his beer and set the mug on the bar.

"Okay." He fidgeted with some change and laid it on the counter next to his empty glass. "I'll do it."

"Friend, you seem...uneasy." The stranger's gaze pierced Morgan's own. "I can't afford to take on someone who may have second thoughts. If that might be the case, I'll leave now and you'll forget we ever had this conversation."

Morgan cleared his throat again. "No second thoughts. I'm your man."

"Excellent." He handed Morgan a cell phone. "Keep it charged. I'll contact you with the details."

"Understood."

"Good. And friend?"

"Yeah?" Morgan looked around the bar. Several men he knew were shooting pool. A couple others had started a poker game at a corner table. No one was watching him. His pulse thrummed in his ears. Nerves.

"You cross me, and you end up in a body bag."

CHAPTER NINE

After an hour of trying on and discarding various outfits, pretty much every garment Annie owned was scattered across her floor in disarray. What exactly did one wear to a barbecue at the McCray ranch? Especially if one wanted to look sexy enough to make Dallas McCray swallow his tongue? She considered calling Dusty, but thought that would make her look completely hopeless.

Which, of course, she was.

The June day was sunny and warm with a spring breeze gently blowing. She finally decided on a dusty violet silk camisole that brought out her eyes—Dallas loved her eyes— and paired it with a floral broomstick skirt that fell nearly to her ankles. She had reapplied her signature toenail polish the evening before, and strappy silver sandals completed her outfit. Dallas loved her feet.

She laughed to herself. How completely absurd. Trying to accentuate every part of her that Dallas had professed to love would make her look like a two-bit whore. Too bad she didn't have see-through magenta pasties to bring out the plum color of her nipples. That would really drive him crazy.

She whirled around in front of the mirror. The creamy silk fell around her full breasts in soft curves, and the rayon skirt lay nicely over her smooth rump. Perfect.

Underneath she wore a lacy demi-bra and a satin thong.

Yes. She, Annie DeSimone, was wearing a thong. The only

thong she owned. The thong she'd had since her bachelorette party and had never worn. The thong she had almost thrown in the good will bag before she left New Jersey.

It rode up her crack, but what the hell.

Dallas McCray, eat your heart out.

Of course, he wouldn't see the thong, but it made her feel sexy. Actually, it made her feel completely underdressed, but Frederick's of Hollywood and Victoria's Secret couldn't be wrong, could they? She'd start to feel sexy soon. As soon as she got used to the feeling of a string flossing her butt cheeks.

Next, she styled her hair, pulling the unruly curls into a mass at the back of her head. She secured it with a butterfly clip and chose a pair of sterling hoop earrings. A little lipstick and blush. Her heavily lashed eyes didn't require mascara, and she hated foundation and powder. Luckily her creamy complexion was nearly flawless and required little enhancement.

She took a deep breath and picked up her pocketbook and the bottle of wine she had bought for Dusty.

It's now or never, Annie.

As she drove to the ranch, she wondered briefly if Joe would be there. Probably not. He hadn't indicated that he was at all close to the McCrays. He probably would have mentioned it to her if he was going, maybe even invited her along. They had shared coffee and tea again yesterday, and although he hadn't kissed her, he'd made it clear that he wanted to see her again.

He was a nice guy. Very intelligent and attractive. Fun to be with. But no sparks. At least not for her.

Dallas, on the other hand, could ignite a forest fire with the sparks he generated in her.

Halfway there she almost turned around. Her heart

was thundering so fast she thought she might have a panic attack. She breathed deeply and willed her body to relax. A few minutes later, she decided relaxation was a little too much to hope for, and she settled for anxious nausea. At least the hyperventilation had stopped.

When she arrived, Seraphina greeted her at the door. "Everyone's out back, Dr. Annie." She took the bottle of wine. "I'll make sure Miss Dusty knows you brought this."

"Thanks, Seraphina," Annie said. "When can we get together and cook some Italian?"

"Anytime, anytime. How about tomorrow? Miss Dusty's brother will still be here."

"It's a date. I'll come by around four, okay?"

"Better make it three," Seraphina said, "for the spices to soften and blend."

"You're absolutely right. Three it is. Are you coming out to join the party?"

"In a bit. After everyone has arrived."

"Great. I'll see you then."

When Annie walked into the back, she was relieved to see that she was dressed appropriately.

"Annie," Dusty called to her. "Over here."

Beside Dusty stood a very tall and attractive man with sandy brown hair. "This is my brother, Sam," Dusty said. "Sam, Dr. Annie DeSimone."

"Dusty's told me a lot about you." He held out his hand.

"It's nice to meet you." Annie took his hand. Strong grip. No spark. Bummer for Dusty's plan.

"Hey, dog." The happy drawl of Chad McCray echoed behind Annie. Although he was the youngest McCray, he was the tallest, and his hair was dark brown, not black like Dallas and Zach's. His facial features were similar though. Grade A stud, like the others.

"Chad, you know Annie?" Sam said.

"Sure he does," Dusty said. "They met at the Bay ranch."

"You're lookin' good, Doc," Chad said. "Can I get you something to drink?"

"Uh, sure," Annie said.

"We've got soda, water, iced tea, beer," Dusty said. "We'll have wine with dinner."

"Iced tea'll be fine for now," Annie said.

"I'll be right back," Chad said, giving her arm a squeeze.

"I see you've caught his eye," Sam said, smiling.

"Not really. We've only met once."

"That's all it takes for Chad. He does like the pretty ladies." Sam took a drink of his beer.

Annie curled her lips upward into a smile that she hoped didn't look too fake. She wished she had asked Chad for a beer. She saw him returning with her iced tea, and then jumped as something nudged her from behind. She turned to see Dallas's dog, Jet, sniffing her. "Hey, fella," she said, kneeling down to pet his happy face.

"Here you are." Chad leaned down to hand her the drink. "You know this mutt?" He gave Jet's ears a squeeze.

"Sure. It's Jet. Dallas's dog."

"Oh." Chad's eyes widened for an instant. "Yeah, he's a good boy. I've got his sister from the same litter."

"Really? I'd love to meet her sometime."

"Anytime. She's great. Her name's Marnie. In fact, she's due for an annual. I'll bring her in to see you next week."

"I'll be glad to look at her," Annie said. "I love all animals, but dogs are my favorite."

"Don't tell anyone, because I'm the resident horse and cattle expert on the McCray ranch, but they're my favorite too." His smile caused cute little crinkles around his brown eyes. "Uh-oh."

"What?"

"Don't look now, but we're getting the evil eye."

"What are you talking about?"

"Dallas. Behind you."

Annie scoffed and rolled her eyes. "Dallas is hardly my concern."

Chad's full lips twisted into a lazy grin. He reached toward her and softly stroked her upper arm with one finger. "I'm right glad to hear that, Dr. Annie."

Annie smiled. "I've heard you're the biggest flirt in the four corner states, Chad."

"Nah." He chuckled and tipped her chin forward. "Only in Colorado and New Mexico combined."

They laughed easily together. Sam and Dusty had joined another group of guests and she and Chad were alone. She gave Jet another scratch behind his ears and drained her iced tea glass. She handed it to Chad. "I think I'll have a beer now."

"Wise choice, Dr. Annie. Wise choice." His eyes gleamed. "I'll be right back."

Annie knelt back down to focus on Jet. "Where's your papa, sweetheart?" she cooed to him.

"Right here."

The sexy low drawl poured over her like a creamy chocolate-raspberry syrup. She stood up and turned to face Dallas.

"Hi," she said.

"Sorry if he's bothering you."

"Jet? He's no bother. You know I love him."

"Not Jet." Dallas's voice cracked. She could tell he tried to hide it, but Annie noticed. "Chad."

"Chad? Why would he be a bother?"

"He...uh, well he..."

"He what, Dallas?"

"He's not serious about women."

"So? From what I've seen, neither are you."

Dallas's grip on his beer bottle tightened, whitening his knuckles. "Maybe I should be talking to him, not you."

"Whatever." Annie smiled when Chad rejoined them and handed her a beer. "Thanks, Chad."

"Not a problem." He turned to Dallas. "You movin' in on my date, big brother?"

"Your date?" Dallas's lips formed a thin line on his taut face.

Ha! Good for you, Chad, Annie thought. Heck no, they weren't on a date, but she wasn't about to clue Dallas in on that fact at this particular moment.

"Well," Chad drawled, "not technically, I suppose, but a guy can always hope."

Annie smiled at him. "Chad's going to introduce me to Marnie. He says she's Jet's sister." She gave Jet another quick pet.

"Great," Dallas said tersely.

"How about tomorrow, Dr. Annie? I'll pick you up around noon and we can have lunch at my place."

Annie opened her mouth to reply, but before any words came out, Dallas grabbed Chad's arm.

"We need to talk, little brother." He pulled Chad away and Annie was left standing alone, beer in one hand, dog ear in the other. She was sure her face had gone completely red.

★ ★ ★

"What the fuck do you think you're doing?" Dallas demanded. "She's not your type at all."

"Hmm." Chad scratched his head. "Beautiful. Intelligent. Funny. *Built*. You're right. What was I thinking?"

Dallas's insides clenched at the thought of his brother's hands on Annie's perfect body. Nope, wasn't going to happen.

"She's too old for you."

"She can't be a day over twenty-six or twenty-seven, Dallas."

"It just so happens she's thirty."

"So what? Older women are delicacies to be savored, brother."

Nausea crept into Dallas's gut as he regarded the lecherous look on his brother's face.

"Besides," Chad continued, "I'm twenty-eight. It's not like she'd be robbing the cradle or anything."

"Stay away from her."

"Why? Have you got some kind of claim on her?"

Damn right I do.

He inhaled sharply. "Just leave her alone, Chad. She just got out of a divorce."

"Then maybe she's up for some fun. I can't say I'd mind a little fun with her. She's gorgeous. And that body. Damn."

Dallas's fists clenched. He was a hair's breadth away from knocking his baby brother unconscious.

"I don't want you with her."

"Are you two...together or something?"

Dallas inhaled and held his breath for a moment. He let the air out of his lungs slowly. "No."

"Then this ain't your business."

"Chad—"

"Look, if you don't want her, there's a slew of cowboys around here who'll be drooling over her in no time. Sam's already got an eye for her, and Joe Bradley, too."

Dallas stiffened. Every hair on his body pressed upward. His teeth ground together and he fought an overwhelming desire to punch the wall.

"You saw her with Joe Bradley?"

"Yeah. Yesterday. They were having coffee at Rena's."

Again? Coffee twice?

"Damn her. She doesn't even like coffee!" Dallas raised his fist.

"Put that down now, Dallas." Chad's voice was even and serious. "I haven't done anything to incur your wrath, and neither has Joe Bradley. If you want the lady, I'll bow out politely, but if not, well—"

"Damn it," Dallas said under his breath.

"I see." Chad adjusted his Stetson. "Enjoy your evening, big brother. Alone. Now if you'll excuse me, there's a pretty filly waiting for me outside."

Dallas seethed. This was more than his heart could take. Already he felt his body preparing to fight for his woman. What the hell was wrong with him? He was civilized. A cowboy. A gentleman. Not some Neanderthal grappling for a mate. Whatever the problem, he couldn't go back out there and watch his brother seduce his Annie.

No. Not *his* Annie. *You don't want her, remember?*

Irritated, he walked to Zach's study, thinking he'd be

alone. Wrong again. Zach was there, finishing up a phone call.

"Sorry," Dallas said, but Zach motioned him inside as he said goodbye to whoever was on the line.

"I'm done. Did you need something in here?"

"Just a respite," Dallas said.

"From a certain pretty veterinarian?" Zach's unique eyes smiled.

"Damn. Am I that transparent?" Dallas plunked into one of the leather armchairs across from Zach's desk.

"'Fraid so. You seemed to be getting along great last weekend. What happened?"

"It's complicated."

"How so?"

"Well, she's divorced."

"Last time I checked, so are you."

"I just found out something she did that I'm having trouble accepting."

"Which is?"

He sighed. "She lied to her husband about something. Something important."

"Do you know the circumstances?"

"No. I didn't ask, and I don't want to know. I'm not getting involved with another deceptive female. I can't make that mistake again. I never make the same mistake twice."

"Annie is nothing like Chelsea."

"How can you be so sure?"

"Well, for one thing, I can stand to be in the same room with her. No offense, but that was never true of your wife."

"You all hated her. I know. But you hated me as well."

"I never hated you, Dallas."

"Okay. Disliked me immensely then."

"How about tolerated with disfavor?"

"Ha. Funny."

"Dallas, you've changed. You're not the same man you were. You've stopped being so mind-numbingly unbearable."

"Thanks." He rolled his eyes.

"Look, Chad and I know Pa was hard on you. He made you a man before you were ready, and he saddled you with a lot of the responsibility for the two of us. That couldn't have been easy, and hell, Chad and I sure didn't make it any easier on you. So I don't blame you for how it used to be." He chuckled. "Especially now that you've unloaded Chelsea."

"Should've done that years ago."

"You'll get no argument from me." Zach absently rubbed his goatee.

"Yeah, I should have, but I didn't. I knew it wasn't working. Hell, it was apparent within the first year or so. But I didn't want to fail, Zach. And I didn't want to admit I'd made a mistake by marrying her in the first place. I still hate myself for it."

"Marriage is a two-way street, Dallas. She helped you fail. You can't shoulder all the blame."

Dallas sighed. Zach was right, but Dallas had still failed, and if he got involved with another woman who was capable of lying to him, he might fail again. "Whatever."

"Can't you give Dr. Annie a chance?"

Dallas inhaled and raked his fingers through his thick hair. "Part of me wants to hold onto her and never let her go."

"That's the part I'd listen to, brother."

"But it's complicated."

"Nah. It's really not." Zach walked toward the door. "Stay here and hide if you want. I've got to get back outside or

Dusty'll have a fit. Besides, I'm on critter duty for a while."

"I'll be glad to look after him for you."

"That's okay. You stay here and mope." Zach shook his head and chuckled as he walked off.

Dallas wasn't sure how long he stayed in Zach's office. Various guests passed by the door, some poking their heads in to say a quick hello. He sat in Zach's leather desk chair, his hands behind his head, feet on the desk, wondering what the hell to do, when a rustling of silk and rayon whisked by the door, followed by a subtle breeze laced with hints of coconut and tulips.

Annie.

"He's too young for you," Dallas called out. He thought for a moment that she hadn't heard him, but then her burgundy highlighted head of curls peeked into the office.

"Did you speak to me?"

Damn, that biting Jersey accent was unbelievably adorable. "Yeah. I said he's too young for you."

"Chad? He's twenty-eight."

"And you're thirty. That would make you a cougar."

"A thirty-year-old woman and a twenty-eight-year-old man is hardly the stuff of scandal, Cowboy. I mean, Dallas." She entered the office and looked around. "Harvard, huh?" she said, looking at Zach's BA and MBA. "I hear you're a Yale man."

"Yeah."

"Okay. Well, see you around."

"Don't get involved with Chad."

Annie turned back around and faced Dallas. Her violet eyes darkened to a soft aubergine. "I don't see the problem. Why shouldn't I date your brother? You've made it painfully obvious that you don't want me."

Dallas rose and walked to the door and shut it. "That's where you're wrong, Annie. I want you so much I'm burning inside." His body was on fire. His gaze seared into her flesh.

Annie backed away, her hands fumbling for something behind her. "Then I fail to see why you've been avoiding me like the plague."

"It's complicated."

"That's a coward's answer, Cowboy." Her voice cracked, but remained steady. "You held me in my bed that first night when I needed you. The next night you made love to me so many times I lost count. I told you I don't sleep around, but I slept with you. I don't regret it, and I didn't think you did either. Until breakfast on Sunday."

"I can't talk about this right now, Annie." He advanced toward her, like an animal stalking his mate.

"Then there's nothing to..."

He fingered a curl that had come loose from her clip.

"Oh God. Don't do this." Her violet eyes smoldered and her lips trembled.

Yeah, she wanted him as much as he wanted her.

"Don't do what?"

"Don't... Not unless you mean it."

He reached behind her and pulled the butterfly clip out of her hair. Her dark tresses curled over her shoulders, down her back. "You look like a gypsy princess." He breathed in and out. Her fragrance intoxicated him. Flowers and coconut, like a tropical beach. Had anything ever smelled so good? So right? "So beautiful." He traced his fingers around one of her silver hoop earrings. "My gypsy princess." He let his hand wander down her cheek, down the smooth lines of her neck and shoulder, down the soft curve of her breast. Her nipple hardened under his touch.

"Oh, damn," she said.

The tension in her body matched his own. Tension they could only ease with each other. "Kiss me, Annie."

"No."

"Yes." He cupped her soft ivory cheek and lowered his head.

"Please." She shook her head, her soft curls tickling his hand. "Don't."

He ignored her, clamped his mouth onto hers, and kissed her, determined to drain all he could from her. He thrust his tongue into her moist warmth, taking her taste, her softness. He was ferocious in his passion. No longer thinking, he let his body guide him. And his body wanted to possess her.

Badly.

He lifted her into his arms and set her down on the leather couch alongside one wall. She stretched out beneath him and he lay on top of her, thrusting his fully clothed erection against her softness. "I can't think of anything but you," he said, rasping. "You never leave me. You haunt my dreams, so there's no peace even in sleep." The soft breath of her moans tickled his cheeks. "Why did you do this to me? Why?"

"Do what? I haven't done—" She stopped, gasping for air, and he took her mouth again.

"I've never felt like this before," he said, panting, after tearing his mouth from hers again. "I can't be with you, but I can't stop desiring you. Your beautiful body. Your sweet lips."

"Why can't you be with me?"

Dallas didn't answer.

"It's all right, Cowboy."

She threaded her fingers through his hair and lightly massaged his scalp. She was trying to soothe him. But it wouldn't work. It would never work.

"What's the matter?"

"What's the matter? Right now I want nothing more than to take your body with mine. This isn't normal."

"It's just...what you said the other night." She puffed against his neck. "Chemistry."

"Right. Chemistry." He tore her silk camisole down the front and ripped her bra from her beautiful breasts. He groaned as he latched on to a dark, turgid nipple.

"What... What am I going to wear home?"

"Who cares?" he said against her chest and devoured her other nipple.

When the sensitive skin of her breasts was ruddy from his beard stubble and her nipples deep purple from his sucking, he turned her over and lifted her skirt. A thong. Sweet God. He cupped the smooth creamy skin of her behind and massaged her. She moaned, little purrs of contentment.

"You have such a sweet little bottom, Annie," he said, "and this thong. It's driving me crazy."

"Get rid of it then." Her voice was low and husky.

Within seconds, he had ripped off the undergarment and tossed the shreds to the floor. "I'm going to take you now. Like this." He smoothed his hands over her back and down over her creamy bottom again. "I want to possess you. Mark you. I want to make you mine. Do you understand me?"

He unbuckled his belt and lowered his jeans and boxers. She lay on the couch, belly down, her pretty face smashed and distorted on the leather. "Please—" she said. "Not like this. Let me turn around—"

"Turn around?"

"Yes," she panted. "I...can't do it like this."

He loved doggy style, but he wouldn't take any woman without her consent. Especially not Annie. *His Annie.* He rolled her gently onto her back and thrust into her.

She groaned and raised her hips to meet him. "God, Cowboy. Please."

He ground his pelvis into hers. "I want you so much, Annie. So much." He plunged into her and felt the edge of her womb against his cock. "I can't think of anything else." Thrust. "I'm hard all the time." Thrust. "I can't eat. I can't sleep." Thrust. "Help me. Help me get over you." Thrust.

Annie sobbed into his shoulder. She spoke, but Dallas couldn't make out the words. He pushed into her heat again and again, raining kisses on her neck and cheeks in rhythm with his thrusts. When she cried out in climax, he shuddered with his own release.

He lay on top of her for a few moments, listening to her breathing, enveloped in her soothing presence. If only...

His cell phone brought him abruptly back to reality. He didn't take the call, but he stood, pulled up his boxers, and refastened his jeans and belt.

"Go," he said.

"Go where? You ripped my top. I... I..." Her eyes misted with tears.

He felt like a monster. He shouldn't have touched her. Now it would be harder for both of them. The urge to cradle her in his arms overwhelmed him. But he'd be strong.

"I'm so sorry, Annie." He sank to the couch and buried his head in his hands. "Please. Just go."

"Fine." She sniffed, holding the two sides of her shorn

blouse together. "Do me a favor though."

"What?"

"Don't you dare ever touch me again." She walked away and slammed the door behind her.

Dallas curled into the couch, inhaling the smoky aroma of the leather mixed with Annie's spicy tropical fragrance. A tear formed in the corner of his eye, but he abruptly stopped it.

He had learned a long time ago that crying was a waste of time.

★ ★ ★

Annie ran straight to her car. If anyone saw her, she wasn't aware of it. Tears streamed down her cheeks as she drove home, her blouse in tatters.

To be taken so forcefully had scared her at first. Had been too much like... But then her feelings had changed. All thoughts except one had flown from her mind. Suddenly her world had become Dallas, as he thrust into her, wanting her, touching her, desiring her in a boundless passion. It had been beautiful. A perfect melding of two bodies, two hearts, two souls.

For her at least.

She had promised herself she'd never cry over a man again, and here she was less than two weeks in Colorado and she'd broken her vow.

It was best to stay away from the McCrays from now on. Unfortunately, that meant no friendship with Dusty, no cooking with Seraphina, and no lunch with Chad tomorrow. She'd call and leave him a message when she got home. He'd be at the party until late, so she could leave an innocuous voice mail on his home line.

By the time she drove into the alley behind the clinic, she had figured it all out. No more McCrays.

Still holding her torn blouse together, she reached for her key and inserted it into her deadbolt. She was astonished to find it unlocked.

"Hi, hon."

Racked with surprise, she dropped both her hands, exposing her well-used breasts to her mother's startled gaze.

CHAPTER TEN

Sylvia DeSimone's blue gaze raked over her daughter's body, lines of worry etched on her delicate features. "What on earth happened to you? Are you all right?"

"Yes, I'm fine, Ma. How did you get in here?"

"I called your landlord. He let me in." Her mother rose and touched Annie's face. "You've been bawling. And considering the state of your clothes, you can understand my concern."

"No concern needed. I wasn't attacked. Or raped. Or any other horrible thing. I promise." Though standing with her breasts fully exposed, not to mention commando under her skirt, she understood how anyone would think otherwise. She kissed her mother's cheek lightly. "I'm fine. Really. Let me go change and I'll be right with you."

In her bedroom, Annie chucked the ruined camisole into the wastebasket. One of her favorite blouses. Damn Dallas McCray anyway. It wasn't enough that he broke her heart. He had to take her clothing as well? She stripped off her skirt and went into the bathroom to clean up and splash some cold water on her face. Then she stepped into some comfortable running shorts and a tank top. Barefoot, she padded back out to her living area where her mother waited.

"Now what is going on, Annalisa?"

"I met a man, is all. I like him a lot. I mean *a lot.*" She sniffed back a sob. "I thought the feeling was mutual, but it turns out he was just after sex. Just like all the other men in the world."

"I'm sorry, hon."

"I've lived through worse."

Sylvia cleared her throat. "I know you have. More than you should ever have had to."

"Yeah." Annie didn't want to rehash old news. "How's Pop?"

"He's good. Misses you."

"I miss both of you too."

"I knew it'd be hard to have you gone, but in a way, I'm glad you're out here." Sylvia lowered her gaze. "I came here to tell you something."

"Tell me something? There's such a thing as a phone you know."

"I didn't want to tell you this over the phone, Annie."

"All right." Annie sat down on the couch next to her mother. "What is it?"

"It's Riggs. He was granted parole yesterday."

"Parole? This soon?"

"Apparently he's been a model prisoner."

Annie breathed deeply, willing herself to relax. It didn't work. "So he finally learned how to behave."

"Evidently. But Annie, there's no need for you to worry. He can't leave the state of New Jersey. If he does, he violates his parole and they send him back to the slammer. There's also the restraining order."

"Ma, you know as well as I do that a crummy piece of paper will never stop Logan Riggs."

"I know. But hopefully the threat of being sent back to prison will."

"I can't let him run my life. He doesn't know where I am.

Who would think to look in this Podunk place anyway?"

"I can't help but worry a little, Annie."

"I know. But don't. Everything'll be fine. Now, it's still early and I haven't eaten. Can I fix you something?"

"Let's go out. My treat. What's good around here?"

"I haven't the foggiest. The only places I've been are the coffee shop and the mechanic. You wouldn't believe how busy it is for a vet here."

"Of course it is. This is a ranching town." Sylvia stood. "You want to change into something more dressy?"

"Heck no. Bakersville's not that kind of town." She stood up and grabbed her pocketbook. "Let's walk down Main Street and see what we can find."

★ ★ ★

The next day, Annie and her mother sat at the Blue Bird Inn perusing the menu for lunch. The Blue Bird was the only business open on Sundays in Bakersville, and Annie had decided to treat her mother to lunch and then drive her to the airport for her five p.m. flight.

Surprisingly, she had enjoyed the short visit with Sylvia. "What looks good, Ma?"

"I should have some of this great Colorado beef I've heard about," Sylvia said, "but it's too early for a steak."

"A burger then. Try the Angus." Annie's cell phone buzzed against her hip. "Excuse me for a minute, will you? It could be a sick animal."

"Don't you get a day off?"

"Not around here." She flipped her phone open. "This is

Annie."

"Hey, Dr. Annie. You on your way?"

"Excuse me?"

"It's Chad McCray. You were coming for lunch today? It's twelve-thirty so I thought I'd see what's keeping you."

Damn. She had come home last night, found her mother, and completely forgotten to cancel her lunch date with Chad and her cooking date with Seraphina.

"I'm so sorry, Chad. When I got home last night, my mother was here for a surprise visit, and I'm afraid I forgot about everything else."

"Bring her along then."

"We're sitting in the Blue Bird. She wants to try Colorado beef."

"You ordered yet?"

"No. Not yet."

"Then don't. I've got the best Colorado beef right here. I'll expect you in half an hour."

"Uh, Chad, I don't think—"

"No arguments." His husky voice was a lot like Dallas's. "I'll see you soon."

Annie rolled her eyes. "I forgot about a lunch date I had."

"Oh?"

"Yeah." She sighed. "Well, you wanted Colorado beef. Let's go."

"Where are we going?"

"A ranch."

"Is this the guy you were telling me about?"

"No. Not exactly."

"What do you mean not exactly?"

"Actually, it's his brother."

"Annalisa, what in God's name have you gotten yourself into?"

"I don't know, Ma. I surely don't know."

The ride to Chad's was pleasant, and Annie was able to show her mother some of the most beautiful scenery in the whole United States. When they arrived, Annie was pleasantly surprised to see Zach and Dusty were there along with Sean. The more buffers between her and Chad, the better.

After she had introduced her mother to everyone, Dusty pulled her aside.

"What happened to you last night?" she asked. "You didn't stay for dinner. I was worried about you. So was Chad."

"I'm sorry. I should have said goodbye before I left." *But I wasn't prepared to expose my breasts to half of Bakersville.* "It was rude of me. I...er..." Of course, her mother was a perfect excuse. "I got a phone call from my mother. She flew in unannounced to see me. So of course I had to go."

"I understand. You could have brought her to the party after you picked her up."

"I didn't want to impose."

"You'll never be an imposition, Annie."

"That reminds me, actually. My mother's leaving tonight, and I need to drive her to the airport. Seraphina and I were supposed to get together and cook. Could you let her know I can't make it?"

"Sure. No problem." Dusty looked at her quizzically. "Is everything all right? You seem a little...off."

"I'm okay."

"Do you want to talk?"

"I can't leave my mother alone with Chad and Zach."

"Heck, she'll be fine. The two of them can make anyone

feel welcome."

"No, it wouldn't be right." But Annie did need to talk to someone, and Dusty was her only friend in Bakersville. "Can we talk tonight?"

"Sure. You want to come by after you drop off your mom?"

"Dusty, that'd be great. Thank you."

"No problem. Now, let's go have lunch with these handsome men."

Annie smiled. Such a sweet girl. Lucky her. She'd snagged the nice brother.

★ ★ ★

"What is it?" Dallas asked his ranch foreman, Tuck Taylor.

"I've got a few dead cattle here, and several more sick ones. I've already asked around. It just started today."

"Shit. All right, let me have a look."

The dead cattle carcasses lay in a cluster, close together. The sick ones were frothing at their mouths and twitching. "Look over there, Tuck," Dallas said, motioning. "A few of them are staggering."

"That's how these started, boss."

"Jesus. What the hell is going on?" He moved toward a dead steer and ran his hands over the flanks. "Wait. This one's breathing," he said. "He's in a coma." He turned to another. "So's this one." One more. "This one's dead, though."

"I'm thinking you should call the vet, Dallas."

Annie? The person he wanted to see most in the world, and the person he didn't want to see most in the world. The duel inside him was exhausting. Slow, painful torture. "I'll call Chad. He'll know what to do."

★ ★ ★

"I've never had a better steak, Mr. McCray," Sylvia DeSimone said, wiping her mouth on her napkin. "And I love this western hospitality. People aren't nearly this friendly in Jersey, are they, hon?"

Annie laughed. "Only if they owe you money. Of course they avoid you like the plague in that case, but they're pretty friendly when they run into you."

Beethoven interrupted their meal. Chad pulled his cell phone out of his pocket and looked at it. "Dallas," he said. "The fool can wait."

"It might be important, Chad," Dusty said.

"On a Sunday afternoon? There's no such thing."

"There goes mine," Zach said, reaching for his cell. "Dallas. I wonder what's going on?"

"Who cares?" Chad said.

"I tend to agree." Zach ignored the call.

"Unreal," Annie said, as her phone vibrated against her hip. She recognized Dallas's cell phone number. "You're never going to guess."

"Dallas," Chad and Zach said in unison.

"I have to take it. He might have a sick animal." Why else would he be calling her? "I'm sorry. Will you excuse me?"

"Sure, Dr. Annie," Chad said. "Tell him to go jump in the lake for me, will you?"

"Gladly," Annie said under her breath as she walked into the kitchen. "This is Annie."

"Hey, Annie, I'm real sorry to bother you."

"What do you want, Dallas?"

"It's...well, I've got some dead steers, and some more real sick ones. Hell, we can afford to lose a few, but disposal of the bodies is expensive, and a pain."

"Cut the crap," Annie said. "I'll be right there. Tell me this, though. Why'd you call Zach and Chad before you called me? I'm the goddamned vet, Dallas."

"How do you know... Don't tell me. Your lunch date with Chad." Dallas's husky voice turned icy.

"Yeah. I'm here at his place. Dusty and Zach are here too. Chad and Zach chose to ignore your call."

"Annie, I—"

"Oh, never mind. I'm losing focus. Your animals are more important than this stupid conversation. I'll be there as soon as I can." She ended the call before he could say anything more.

She walked back into the dining room. "I have to go," she said. "Dallas has some dead cattle and some sick ones. It doesn't sound too good." She sighed. "Ma, I don't know how long this'll take. Thankfully my vet bag's in the car, but—"

"Don't worry, hon. I'll just call a cab. That's how I got to your place yesterday."

"That must have been a hell of an expensive fare," Annie said.

"It's fine. Don't worry. This is your job, Annie."

"I'll take you, Mrs. DeSimone," Zach said. "Chad and Dusty should go with Annie. They're good with animals. That leaves me and the critter as your escorts."

"Oh, I couldn't impose."

"It's not an imposition. You're great company." Zach flashed a winning smile. "You don't mind, do you, darlin'?" He nodded to Dusty.

"It's a perfect plan," Dusty agreed. "Let's go see to the cattle."

"I'm sorry about this, Ma." Annie bent to kiss her mother's cheek. "I'm so glad you came. Next time for longer, okay?"

"And for a more pleasant reason, I hope," Sylvia said. "Okay, if you don't mind taking me, Mr. McCray, I'd appreciate it."

"Not at all. And call me Zach."

"Okay." She stood and embraced Annie. "I love you, hon. Go do your job."

After Annie had transferred her mother's carry-on to Zach's pickup, she and Dusty followed Chad's truck to Dallas's cattle barn. Dallas and several other men were huddled around a convulsing steer. Annie grabbed her bag and headed toward them, Chad and Dusty close behind. She touched Dallas's upper arm gently.

When he turned, the look of anguish on his handsome face startled Annie. Here was a man who truly cared about his animals and hated to see them suffer. It took every ounce of self-control she possessed not to throw herself into his arms.

Instead, she told them all to move back so she could have a look. Dallas didn't bother introducing her to his ranch hands, and she wasn't interested in their names at the present. Not when a creature was suffering.

The steer's legs were twitching slightly, and his mouth was covered in slimy froth. He was clearly fighting for every breath. "Dallas," she said, without looking up, "you need to have your men remove all the healthy cattle from this ranging site. Any that are staggering or look otherwise ill, leave here."

"Yeah, yeah, okay. Tuck, take care of that will you please?"

"Sure thing. You all heard the boss," the man called Tuck said, "let's get these head moving."

"There's not much I can do for him right now," Annie said. "My best bet is to look at a dead one."

"Okay, okay." Dallas led her to a carcass. Chad and Dusty followed.

Annie had a hunch. She didn't like it, but she had to check it out. She pulled a scalpel out of her bag.

"What are you going to do, Annie?" Dusty asked.

"I'm going to cut him open."

"Why?"

"I need to see his blood."

She put on a pair of rubber gloves and made a small incision on the steer's neck, near the carotid artery. She inserted her fingers into the incision. The blood against the white rubber was a bright reddish orange.

"Damn," Dallas said. "That's not normal, is it?"

"No, bro," Chad said. "It's not. Annie, are you thinking what I'm thinking?"

"If you're thinking cyanide poisoning, then yeah." She stripped off the gloves and put on a clean pair. "You got any enemies, Dallas?"

CHAPTER ELEVEN

Dallas stood, mouth agape.

"I'll need to run some tests, but I'm pretty sure these cattle have been poisoned."

"How?" Dallas asked.

"Any number of ways. Sometimes from the grass they eat."

"Cattle have been eating this grass for decades," Dallas said.

"True, but you're coming out of a drought," Annie said.

"So?"

"So, Dallas," Chad said, "drought puts stress on the plants, particularly sorghum grass, which produces cyanide. This is re-growth, too."

"Which increases the risk," Annie said. "We'll need to test these grasses, but honestly, I don't think that's the problem."

"Why?" Chad asked.

"You've been coming out of a drought for several years," Annie said. "If these grasses were producing cyanide, you would have seen evidence of it before now."

"Makes sense," Chad agreed.

"What else do you feed them?" Annie asked.

"We use a special mixture of corn and other grains that Chad came up with," Dallas said. "He just mixed up a new batch a few days ago."

"Yep, I sure did," Chad said.

"Is it possible that someone could have poisoned the grain?" Annie asked.

"No," Dallas said. "Absolutely not. All my men have been with me for years."

"Hmm." Annie looked around at the dying animals. "When were they last fed the grain?"

"This morning."

"What time this morning?"

"I don't know. We don't keep to an exact schedule."

"A steer can die within minutes if he eats a lethal dose," Annie said. "It's taking these guys longer, if the grain is the culprit."

"Can you treat the ones that haven't died?"

"I'm afraid it's too late for some of them. The ones that are staggering along, though, we can drench in sodium thiosulphate. They should recover. I have enough for about ten head in my bag. I'll have to return to town for more, and I'll order a huge supply first thing in the morning. You may need it if we can't find the source of the cyanide."

"You really think it's the grain, Annie?" Dusty asked.

"Seems more likely than the grass, even considering the drought. I'll take a sample with me and have it analyzed. In the meantime, Dallas, don't feed them any more of the grain. Let them live on the grass for a few days. If more get sick, we'll know it's the grass and not the grain."

She pulled some packages out of her bag and handed them to Chad. "Sixty grams of this in six hundred milliliters of water. Give it to any that are staggering and looking ill. Don't bother with the ones who are already comatose. It's too late."

Annie pulled a syringe out of her bag and took a sample of the dead steer's blood. She petted him gently on his bristly head. "I'm sure sorry, fella," she said under her breath.

Dallas knelt down beside her.

"You love them all, don't you?"

She nodded, unable to speak for a minute. She hated suffering, especially of innocents. To her, animals were as innocent as newborn babies.

"Animals can't help themselves. I became a vet so I could help them. When I can't..." She blinked back a few tears and took a deep breath. "Well, there's no use crying over it, is there?" She stood up. "Get me a sample of the grain."

Dallas nodded, reached toward her, and caressed her forearm with his thumb. "I'm glad you're here."

Annie brushed the dirt off her knees. "I wish I could have done more."

"You did your best, which is better than any of us could have done." Dallas rose and stood next to her. His fingers grazed hers, and a spark shot through her.

Damn chemistry.

"If you could get me the grain sample..."

"In a minute." He took her hand. The ranch hands were still busy herding the cattle, and Dusty and Chad were dispensing the medication. "Thank you, Annie."

"It's my job, Dallas." She tried to pull her hand out of his, but he held on tight and lowered his head.

"Don't," she said.

"Just one. Please." He released her hand, cupped her face, and brushed his lips lightly over hers.

The sparks rippled across her skin, tightening her nipples and landing between her legs.

"Damn it," she said, shaking loose from his grasp. "Damn you, Dallas McCray. You're not playing fair."

"I'm not playing, Doc."

"It's just chemistry, remember?"

"Yeah. Right." He backed away from her. "I'm sorry."

"No worries. I'll go help Dusty and Chad with the drenching. I'll come around first thing in the morning to check on them."

"Will you have any results on the blood or the grain by then?"

"Probably not. I'll get them as soon as I can though."

"Okay. Thanks, Annie. Thanks an awful lot."

She tried to force a smile, but wasn't sure she was successful. "Like I said, Cowboy, it's my job."

★ ★ ★

The knife again, piercing his flesh, straight to his marrow. Dallas watched Annie walk away, toward Dusty, Chad, and the struggling steers.

Chemistry? Sure, they had that. But this gut-twisting dagger and the sadness in his heart had nothing to do with chemistry.

Dallas was in love. For the first time in his life.

He was in love with Annalisa DeSimone. But he couldn't be with her. He wouldn't allow himself. The fucking knife—it twisted into his flesh with a piercing pain.

Now he only had to figure out what to do about it.

★ ★ ★

Annie helped Dusty prepare dinner. Because Annie had broken her date to cook with Seraphina, the housekeeper had decided to visit her daughter in town.

After they had fed Zach and Sean, Dusty poured two glasses of Chardonnay, and led Annie to her cozy study. She sat down on a brocade sofa and patted the seat next to her. "Girl talk," she said.

Annie sat down and took a sip of her wine. "I don't know where to start."

"At the beginning. Or not at all. It's up to you."

"No, I want to talk. I... I really appreciate your friendship. It's hard, coming to a new place where you don't know anyone."

"I know. I felt the same way. But at least I had Zach."

"He's great, by the way."

"Yeah, he is. And so's Chad. And even Dallas."

Annie nodded.

"So is it Chad?"

Annie shook her head. "No. He's wonderful, a lot of fun. But he's not for me."

"Dallas then."

She nodded. "But he doesn't want me."

"I think you're wrong. What happened?"

"This is hard for me to say. I don't want you to think I'm some slut from New Jersey."

Dusty giggled. "Are there a lot of sluts in New Jersey?"

"More than a few."

"I think you can say that about anywhere. But you're not a slut, Annie. I assume it went pretty far then?"

"You could say that."

"Last weekend?"

"Yeah." She took another sip of wine. "He stayed with me Friday night, just holding me. I actually intended to sleep with him. It was heading in that direction, but we started talking about our divorces, and..."

"Yeah?"

"Well, let's just say the thought of my ex kills the mood for me."

"I see."

"But I didn't want to be alone. I was feeling kind of needy and pathetic. So he stayed. He held me in his arms all night. Then he brought me herb tea in the morning."

"Dallas? Really?" Dusty shook her head. "I always knew he was a nice guy, but that's really sweet."

"Yeah, it was. He took me back to his place that evening, and guess who showed up?"

"Who?"

"His ex-wife."

"Chelsea? You're kidding. Dallas paid her a mint to get rid of her."

"So I've heard. Anyway, after he got rid of her, we had our dinner and then... Well, I don't need to spell it out for you."

"How was it?" Dusty giggled, her eyebrows arched.

"Amazing. The best. We couldn't get enough of each other."

"So what happened?"

"That's what I can't figure out. Everything was great. We made plans to see each other the next night. Then all of a sudden, he backs out."

"That doesn't make any sense."

"It didn't to me either."

"Maybe he's a little skittish because of the divorce."

"Maybe. I don't know. Everything seemed fine until I asked him for my pocketbook."

"What for?"

"To take my birth control pill." Annie widened her eyes,

recalling the conversation. "That was it. The pills."

"What about them?"

"He asked about my marriage, whether we wanted kids. I said my ex did, and so did I, but not with him, so I had stayed on the pill."

"Without his knowledge?"

"Yeah. But I had good reason."

"I'm sure you did. But I think I may see the problem."

"What?"

"I think I need to tell you a little about Dallas's marriage."

"It's not really any of my business."

"I'm thinking it is. This is all starting to make sense, as you'll see in a minute."

"Okay. Shoot."

"Dallas and Chelsea were together for about ten years."

"Really? That long?"

"Yeah. Dallas was never happy, but didn't want to admit failure and end the marriage. At least that's my take on it."

"He tried to be gentlemanly."

"Exactly. You do know him, don't you?"

"Yeah. It's annoying, to tell you the truth."

"A little." Dusty laughed. "Anyway, the straw that broke the camel's back came when he found out Chelsea had been deceiving him."

"How?"

"Well, Dallas wanted kids, and Chelsea said she did, too. According to Zach, they didn't have much of a sex life, so I guess Dallas just thought they hadn't hit the right time yet. Until he found Chelsea's stash."

"Stash of what?"

"Birth control pills. She had been taking them throughout

their entire marriage. Turns out she really didn't want kids. Was afraid pregnancy would taint her perfect body, or something like that."

"Oh, God..."

"So you see, when you told Dallas you were on the pill without your husband's knowledge, that probably brought back the whole ugly mess with Chelsea."

"But, Dusty, I had good reason for not wanting to get pregnant. It had nothing to do with some sainted image of my body."

"Did you tell Dallas that?"

"He didn't ask."

"Do you want to tell me?"

Annie cleared her throat. "I'm not sure."

"You don't have to. But I'm here if you change your mind."

"Thanks. And I do want kids someday."

"They're the best," Dusty said. "I can't imagine my life without Sean. And I may not get the chance to have another."

"Why not?"

"It's a long story."

"You can tell me if you want."

"I don't mind talking about it. I had leukemia when I was eighteen. The chemo affected my fertility. I only menstruate once a year or so, which means I don't ovulate very often. We got lucky with Sean."

"Wow. I'm so sorry."

"It's okay. I have Sean. I have Zach. I'm as happy as I could ever imagine being." She beamed. "And we do our best to hit that once a year jackpot."

"Can't say I blame you. Your husband's a stud." Annie turned serious. "And your illness?"

"It's been nearly seven years now. I'm considered cured."

"Thank God."

"I do. Every morning and every night."

"I can't imagine going through something like that."

"Do you think it's worse than what you went through in your first marriage?"

Annie warmed. Redness seared her chest. "How did you know?"

"We're kindred spirits, Annie. Animal lovers always are. I've seen you with your patients. I know how much you care. I know what a good mother you'd be. If you kept yourself from becoming one, you had a good reason."

"I did."

"You don't need to tell me if you don't want to. But I think you should tell Dallas."

"No."

"Why not?"

"I can't. He... He won't want me anymore. I'm damned if I do and damned if I don't."

"Of course he'll want you. Why wouldn't he?"

"Because...when I think about it... When I think about what I let happen to me... I... Well, I don't really want myself."

"Oh, Annie."

"He went to prison for what he did to me. And now—" Annie gulped back a sob. "Now he's out. That's why my mother flew out unannounced yesterday. She didn't want to tell me over the phone. He's been released on parole."

"Annie, honey, come here." Dusty opened her arms.

"I'm all right. Really." Unshed tears stung her eyelids. She wasn't used to kindness. She loved her family, but they weren't touchers. People in Jersey didn't share their feelings.

She wouldn't. She couldn't.

But she found herself in the arms of her first real friend in a long time, crying her heart out.

★ ★ ★

Logan Riggs needed money. He could make a bundle in the casinos, but he needed some starting cash. The few friends he had were all tapped out. At least that's what they said. His other contacts... well, he'd lost them when he'd fingered them to the cops to help move his parole date along.

Nark. Canary. Squealer. That's what he was. But a free nark. He could live with that.

Now he had to find the only source of green he knew of. His sweet little ex-wife. She had received an inheritance from some old biddy aunt in Italy before he was arrested. Now it was time to collect.

Of course, there was a little problem. He had no idea where she was, and no one was talking. She and her family had a restraining order against him. He'd stay away from her family. They wouldn't tell him anything anyway. They'd die first, all of them.

She, however, was another story. He could control the little bitch. He just had to find her.

He fired up the Internet to have a look, but was temporarily interrupted by his cell phone.

"Riggs," he said roughly.

"Logan Riggs?"

"Yeah. I don't recognize your number. Who is this?"

"I'm a friend. I have some information for you."

"I don't have time for games. I'm on parole, and I need to

find someone."

"I'm aware of your situation, Mr. Riggs. I think we can help each other."

"How's that, *friend*?"

"I know where to find a certain veterinarian you might be looking for."

Riggs cleared his throat and rubbed his arms that had become suddenly chilly. "I'm listening."

"I can tell you where she is," the voice said, "but I want something in return."

"What might that be?"

"I want her hurt. Badly."

"Friend," Riggs said, "I'm your man."

CHAPTER TWLEVE

It wasn't your fault. It wasn't your fault.

The whispered words echoed in Annie's ears. Dusty had repeated them over and over the previous night, rocking Annie as if she were Sean. Annie had sobbed and gasped into her friend's shoulder, eventually pouring out the whole story of her marriage to Riggs and swearing Dusty to secrecy.

When she was all cried out, Dusty had taken her upstairs to a guest bedroom and put her to bed, kissing her forehead like a child's.

This morning, after a quick breakfast, courtesy of Seraphina, she had thanked Dusty profusely and left. Now, after having stopped at her office to send the blood and grain from yesterday to the lab and to pick up more sodium thiosulphate for Dallas's cattle, she was driving to Dallas's ranch. She thanked God for the Colorado sun, necessitating the sunglasses that hid her eyes, red and swollen from crying.

You need to tell Dallas.

Dusty again. As Annie drove up the dirt road toward the ranging site where the sick cattle were gathered, she couldn't shake her friend's words. She'd promised Dusty that she'd consider it, but she knew in her heart she could never tell Dallas. It was too humiliating.

Speak of the handsome devil himself. Dallas stood, with Chad, next to another sick steer. Annie hit the brakes and got out of the car, her vet bag in hand.

"Another one?" she said, walking toward them.

"'Fraid so, Dr. Annie," Chad said. "We must have missed this one yesterday."

Annie sighed and knelt down beside the sick animal. "It's too late for him," she said, shaking her head. "I'm sorry."

She stood up and pulled the medication out of her bag and handed it to Chad. "This is all the sodium thiosulphate I have left. I ordered a ton more this morning, overnight. It'll be here tomorrow. I also sent the blood and the grain to the lab with a rush. Of course they can't guarantee a specific time for the results." She cleared her throat. "In the meantime..."

"Yeah?" Dallas said.

"I think you should contact the authorities."

"The sheriff you mean?"

Annie nodded. "I'm testing the grass, but I don't think it's the culprit. I think someone deliberately poisoned your cattle. We won't have any proof until the grain comes back from the lab, and even then, it could come up negative. But this doesn't seem like an accident to me, Dallas."

"Honestly, it doesn't to me either."

"Is there anyone you can think of who would want to harm you?"

"No one who has access to my grain."

"All right." She glanced around at the other cattle. "The cops will ask you all these questions anyway. Call them now, will you?"

He nodded.

"I'm going to have a look at the rest of these guys."

"Thank you, Annie."

"No need to thank me."

"I think there is."

Annie scoffed. "Wait till you get my bill, Cowboy. Then decide if you want to thank me." She strode toward a staggering steer.

★ ★ ★

"That's about the extent of it," Dallas told Sheriff Doug Cartwright. "I trust all my men. I haven't brought in anyone new in over two years."

"Could any of them be bought off, do you think?" Doug asked.

"Honestly, yesterday I'd have said no way, but after lying awake all last night ruminating, I just don't know, Doug."

"I'll need to speak to the vet. Where is she?"

"She's out with Chad medicating the animals. I'm sure they'll be back shortly."

"I've heard a lot about her. She as cute as the locals say she is?"

There went the knife again, twisting its way through his entrails. Was every man in the four corner states going to hit on his woman? At least Doug was married.

"She's attractive." Dallas's vocal cords were tied in knots. "Here they come now."

"Hey, Doug," Chad said, shaking the sheriff's hand.

"Hey yourself." He turned to Annie and eyed her up and down.

Dallas wanted to hit him. His fingers curled into his palms.

"You must be this famous Dr. Annie I've heard so much about."

"That's me, and you are?"

"Out of uniform, I'm afraid. I'm Doug Cartwright, the county sheriff."

"Nice to meet you."

"I need to ask you some questions about these animals."

"Shoot."

After Annie had told the sheriff all she knew and suspected, she turned to Dallas. "I need to get back. I'll call you if I hear anything from the lab. You too, Sheriff. I'll be by tomorrow morning to have another look."

"Thank you," Dallas said.

"It's my job."

"You going to be around later today?" Doug asked.

"I'll be in my office in town, unless I get a call. Why?"

"Thought you might like to grab a coffee."

Damn. Red anger crept up Dallas's spine. "She doesn't like coffee," he said, "and aren't you married, Doug?"

"I guess you haven't heard. Sandy and I separated two months ago."

"In that case," Annie said, "I'd love to have a coffee."

"For someone who hates coffee, you spend a lot of time in that damn coffee shop," Dallas said through clenched teeth.

"Calm down. I'll have tea. Stop by anytime this afternoon," she said to Doug. "It was nice meeting you."

"Very nice meeting you," Doug said. "I'll see you later today."

"I'll look forward to it." Annie walked to her VW Beetle, got in, and drove away.

"She's some looker," Doug said to Dallas and Chad. "The accent's a little grating, but her body makes up for it."

"I think her accent's charming," Chad said, "and I wholeheartedly agree about her body. You've got some competition for her though."

"You?"

"Maybe. We had lunch yesterday. And Joe Bradley. He's seen her a few times."

"Well, I'm hardly looking for a serious relationship. I'm technically still married. Wouldn't mind a roll in the hay with some of that, though."

Dallas couldn't help himself. He lunged forward and punched the sheriff right in the jaw.

He eyed the redness in his knuckles. His fist felt damn good.

"Are you crazy?" Chad tackled him to the ground. "He's a lawman for Christ's sake."

Doug, clearly stunned, sat on the ground rubbing his jaw. "I could arrest you for that, Dallas."

"Go ahead."

"I'll give you the benefit of the doubt, though, seeing as how you're upset about your stock."

"You treat that lady with respect, Doug, and you'll have no more problems with me."

"You her protector or something?"

"No. Just be good to her."

"Dallas—" Chad began.

"No. Don't say it, Chad."

"This is my exit cue." Doug rose to his feet. "Let me know of any new developments in the case." He wiggled his jaw back and forth. "You pack a mean punch, Dallas. I'll try to remember to stay on your good side."

"You should hit him back," Chad said. "God knows he deserves it."

"Not while I'm on duty, but I might take you up on it some

other time. See you all around."

As the sheriff drove away, Chad turned to Dallas. "It's time for you and me to have a talk, big brother."

"Can't imagine what about."

"You're in love with that woman."

Dallas inhaled sharply. He couldn't deny it. "It's none of your concern."

"You're in love with her all right. I knew the minute Zach fell for Dusty, and I knew the minute you fell for Dr. Annie." He scoffed. "God, the two of you are so transparent it's amusing."

"Like I said, it's not your concern."

"Get it through your thick head, if you haven't already. She's beautiful, and she's built. And even more attractive to the cowpokes around here, she's different. She wears different clothes, a different hairstyle. She even talks differently. She paints her toes silver. Which is really hot, by the way, though God knows why."

Dallas's facial muscles tightened.

Chad continued. "People are going to take notice, Dallas. Hell, you've seen it already."

"And your point is?"

"Whatever's keeping you from her, get over it."

"It's not that simple."

"What is it?"

"This conversation is over."

"Suit yourself. Hear this, though. You came close to taking a swing at me over her yesterday, and you didn't stop yourself with Doug today. You're damn lucky he took it in stride. If you plan to clock every guy who looks Annie's way, prepare to have it come back to bite you in the ass. Sooner rather than later."

"I can control myself. I don't need some twenty-eight-year-old who's never had a serious relationship giving me pointers."

"I'm thinking you're the one who's never had a serious relationship."

"I was married!"

"What difference does that make? You and Chelsea had about as much to say to each other as Jesus and the devil. Though I can't decide which of you is the devil in that analogy." He chuckled. "Marriage is a piece of paper, Dallas. You never loved Chelsea, and she never loved you. But you love Annie. You're a fool to let her go."

"You don't know shit about love, Chad."

"Well...can't say I've ever been in love myself, but I know gut-wrenching, heart-stopping love. I saw it with our parents and with Zach and Dusty. And now with you." He scratched his head. "Course it's not all that attractive in your case."

Dallas sighed. "You don't know the half of it, brother."

"What'd she do that was so bad, Dallas?"

"I don't want to talk about it."

"Suit yourself." Chad adjusted his Stetson. "Not that you deserve it, but I'll leave her alone in deference to your feelings. But don't expect Joe and Doug to share my scruples." He tucked his hands in his pockets. "I've got some work to do. Call me if anything else happens with the stock."

"Will do."

★ ★ ★

Bakersville, Colorado.

That was where Annie was hanging out her shingle.

Some little Podunk town on the back ass of nowhere.

Trying to hide from him, no doubt. She'd soon see how futile that was.

Riggs stopped at a convenience store to fill up his gas tank. He had no credit cards and was running low on cash, so he decided a little hold up was in order. He was alone on the Kansas prairie, and he needed to conserve his resources. This gas was going to be on the store. His revolver, obtained illegally before he left New Jersey, sat idly on the passenger seat next to him. When the gas nozzle clicked, he replaced it on the pump, leaned in over the driver's seat, and picked up his gun.

Behind the counter stood a teenage boy. Kansas farm boy to a tee. Tall, lanky, freckle-faced, and nervous. Riggs walked around the back of the store, casing it. Farm boy seemed to be alone. This was going to be the easiest heist he had ever pulled.

"That'll be thirty-five even, sir, on pump two," the boy said, his gaze not quite meeting Riggs's eyes.

Riggs threw a bag of sunflower seeds on the counter. "How much with these?"

The boy rang up the seeds. "Thirty-seven fifty altogether."

Riggs pulled his revolver from under his shirt. "That'll be on you, freak, and I'll take the rest of the cash you've got."

The boy froze, a slight tremble of his lips the only movement on his glacier like face.

"Did you not hear me, idiot? I said give me your cash."

"I-It's not here. It's in a s-safe. I... I don't have access."

Bullshit. Riggs knew a liar when he saw one. The kid had balls though. He'd give him that. "Get the cash, you clown, or I'll take it out of your hide."

The boy's whole body quivered when Riggs touched the tip of the gun to his forehead. Was he pissing himself?

"P-Please. I don't have access. You've got to believe me."

"Well, I don't. You have thirty seconds to produce the cash, or you can say goodbye to your farm. One, two, three—"

Riggs stared intently as the boy fumbled underneath the counter. Damn! A silent alarm, no doubt. He hadn't considered a tiny farm town store would have such a luxury. Riggs panicked. His blood chilled several degrees in his veins and his pulse raced. Shit, he was going to be sick. What now?

He closed his eyes and fired his revolver, the recoil vibrating up his arm to his shoulder.

He opened one eye and then the other and walked slowly behind the counter. The boy lay still on the floor, one eye shot out. Crimson streams of blood meandered down his cheeks. But that wasn't the worst. The display of snuff and cigarettes behind the counter was spattered with blood and brains. Riggs heaved and his stomach emptied on the dead boy's chest.

Shit. He hadn't wanted to kill the guy. Now what?

Frantic, he looked around for a video camera. He didn't see one, thank God.

He ran out to his car and gunned the engine, determined to put as many miles between him and Tiny Creek, Kansas as he could.

CHAPTER THIRTEEN

Coffee with Doug Cartwright was easy. Annie sat across from the attractive red-haired sheriff. His brown eyes had a natural twinkle, and he had an adorable dimple on his left cheek when he smiled. The sun's rays coming through Rena's front window cast highlights of gold and copper in the auburn mane that fell to his shoulders. And he was funny. He made her laugh.

She thought again how easy he was to be with. A lot like Joe Bradley. Handsome as they both were, though, Annie felt no spark. Damn Dallas McCray anyway. She hadn't felt that kind of spark with any man before him. Certainly not with Riggs, though he had swept her off her feet at one time.

Nope. Not with any man except Dallas. He had ruined her for any other. She just wasn't interested.

"So are you hungry?" Doug's voice jolted her back to reality. "Dana over at the Blue Bird makes a great green chile. We could catch a bite, and maybe a movie."

Annie smiled, though her heart wasn't in it. "Sure. Sounds great."

"Awesome, let's go."

Dana's green chile, while excellent, was spicier than Annie expected. Her skin heated as she grabbed for her glass of water.

"You okay?" Doug asked.

"Yeah, fine," Annie rasped. "Just a little hot for me."

"Sorry, babe. I should have warned you. Don't you have

Mexican in Jersey?"

"Well, we have Taco Bell."

Doug erupted in a peal of laughter. "That ain't Mexican, honey."

"I'm sure I'll get used to it. As soon as the smoke stops coming out my ears." Annie wiped her eyes with her napkin and motioned to their waitress. "More water please."

The waitress laughed and nodded.

"I have a feeling I'm a joke in here tonight," Annie said to Doug.

"Nah. Just a new girl in town, so everybody's interested."

"I guess I've made quite a splash."

"You'd make a splash anywhere, babe. Just look at you."

"Thank you. I think. So what do you want to see tonight?"

"Well, we have a choice. We can check out what's playing at the Plex, or..."

"Or what?"

"We could rent a couple of DVDs and go back to my place."

"Oh." Annie's heart nearly stopped. She wasn't ready to go to his place. "How about the Plex? I haven't been there yet."

"Disappointing choice." He laughed. "But okay. There's all kinds of time for other stuff."

"Just what I was thinking." Her cell phone vibrated. "I'm sorry. Would you excuse me? I have to take it. It might be a sick animal." Good excuse to end the conversation too. "This is Annie," she said into the phone.

"It's me."

Dallas.

"Yeah? What's up? Do you have another sick steer?"

"No. I just wanted to talk to you. To hear your voice."

His words were slightly slurred. Annie excused herself

HELEN HARDT

to Doug and walked to the women's room. "You've been drinking."

"A little." Dallas hiccupped into the phone.

"Look, if you don't have a veterinary emergency, I'm afraid I need to go. I'm kind of in the middle of something."

"What? Hot date?"

Hell. Why not tell him? He probably wouldn't remember in the morning anyway. "Yes, I'm on a date. With Doug Cartwright."

"He's married, Doc."

"He's separated."

"You don't want to get involved with him."

"Yes, yes, I know. Just like I don't want to get involved with Chad."

"Or Joe Bradley," Dallas agreed.

"Of course. Anyone else I should stay away from? Besides you, of course?"

"I don't want you to stay away from me."

"Oh? That's news."

"I want you. I want to kiss your sweet lips. I want to run my tongue over your beautiful nipples and lick down your belly all the way to that sweet, hot—"

Annie squeezed her thighs together as she moistened, her clit throbbing. She wanted him so badly she thought she might implode on the spot. "Stop right there, Dallas. I'll see you in the morning."

"Come over, Doc. Please? I'd come to you but I can't drive. I've had a little bit to drink."

"I'll say. I'll see you in the morning." She clicked the phone off.

She couldn't continue her date with Doug. It wouldn't be

fair to him. Clearly, he had more than just a friendly movie in mind, and she didn't want to lead him on.

"I'm sorry," she said as she sat back down at the table. "I can finish dinner, but I'm going to have to take a rain check on the movie. I need to go on a call."

"Shoot. Well, how about tomorrow night then?"

"Weekdays are bears for me. Can we make it the weekend?"

"I guess you're worth the wait." His brown eyes beamed and he flashed his sexy dimple.

"That's sweet of you. I truly am sorry." And also a liar, but what the heck?

Doug kissed her good night at her door. A lingering open-mouthed kiss that she could have done without. She ended it as quickly as she could and thanked him again for the dinner, assuring him she'd see him on the weekend, but already thinking up ways to break the date.

Inside she plopped on her couch and thought about Dallas. Poor inebriated Dallas who would feel like hell in the morning. Served him right.

Ten minutes later, she was in her car driving to him. A glutton for punishment, that's what she was. After all, she'd stayed with Riggs all those years, hoping things would get better, knowing full well they wouldn't.

Now she was on her way to play nursemaid to a man who clearly wanted her, but didn't want to want her. The thought of him spending the night alone in a drunken stupor was more than she could bear. Even if he did deserve it.

He didn't answer the doorbell. She tried the door but it was locked. Clearly he had learned something from the whole Chelsea debacle. She went around to the back. It was open.

She stole in quietly. The house was dark, which surprised her. "Dallas?" she called. "It's me. I'm here."

She walked up the stairway to his bedroom. There he was, sprawled on his bed, a bottle of Macallan in his hand. The TV was turned to ESPN.

"Dallas?"

His head turned toward the door. "Annie. Oh, thank God!"

He struggled to his feet.

"No, Cowboy, don't get up. I'll come to you."

She took the bottle from him. It was nearly empty. "How full was this when you started?"

"All the way."

She studied it. "Twenty-five year? This stuff's over a hundred dollars a bottle. You should be ashamed of yourself, wasting it."

"I want a kiss," he announced.

"I'm not here for that. I'm here to take care of you."

"Why?"

"Let's just say I owe you one. You took care of me that first night, remember?"

She wasn't sure he'd heard a word she said. "A kiss. Please, Doc. One kiss."

"Personally, I can't stand Scotch, Cowboy, and you'll likely taste like a barrel of it. So I'll pass on the kiss."

"I said I want a kiss." He grabbed her arm, pulled her onto the bed, and rolled on top of her.

"Mmmpphh," Annie said.

His mouth clamped onto hers. She opened to him in spite of herself. Intoxication clearly didn't inhibit his kissing abilities. She moaned into his mouth as his tongue danced around hers. He did taste like Scotch, but it wasn't bad. It wasn't bad at all. Because he also tasted like Dallas. Like the man she loved.

The thought that crept into her mind jerked her out of the kiss. She wasn't in love with him. She couldn't be. *God, he doesn't even want me.* She pushed him away. It wasn't difficult, considering his condition.

"Get off of me," she said, her voice sharp and commanding.

He lay sprawled on the bed again. "I've missed you."

"Have you now?"

"Yeah. I think about you all the time. I can't stop. It's driving me insane." He pulled at his hair. "Even the Scotch doesn't stop it."

"You've had enough Scotch," Annie said.

"Nope. Need more. Need to pass out."

"Oh, you will," Annie said, "but you'll probably have to throw up first."

"Nah. I never throw up. I'm sensible. I don't drink enough to throw up. Never have. Chad and Zach, they threw up. I had to take care of both of them, keep it from our pa. He would've whooped their asses."

"That was you, huh? The sensible big brother?"

"Yep. Always the sensible one. Never made the same"—he hiccupped—"mistake twice."

"All right. No more talking now. I'm going to run you a bath. You need one."

"Only if you get in with me." He pawed for her.

"Not a chance. While the water's filling up I'll go to the kitchen and brew you some coffee. Which you *will* drink, do you hear me?"

"Yes'm."

She took the bottle from the night stand. "This is going in the trash, and you're not to touch any more of the stuff, *capiche*?"

"*Capiche*. That's cute. You're so cute, Doc."

"You're not going to think I'm cute when I get done with you. Stay here."

She started a bath in Dallas's luxurious jetted tub and then went down to the kitchen to make the coffee.

By the time she got back, Dallas was sitting on the side of the bed. "Remember how I said I never throw up?"

"Ugh. Don't tell me. Come on, let's get you to the bathroom. Quickly."

She pulled him off the bed, walked him to the bathroom, and stood him in front of the toilet. "If you don't mind, I'd rather not watch." She closed the door and left the bedroom. She didn't want to hear it either. Ten minutes later, she returned.

"Cowboy?" she said to the door.

"Yeah. I'm done."

"You want me to come in?"

"Just go away and let me die."

Annie laughed in spite of herself. "No, Cowboy, you'll live. Trust me, I know." She opened the door and looked around. "At least you managed to hit the target. That's more than I did my first time." She took his toothbrush from the counter and spread it with toothpaste. "Here you are. Brush like a good boy."

"No."

"Yes."

"Why should I?"

"You want any more kisses?"

"More than I want my next breath of oxygen."

"Then brush. I'm not kissing you unless you do."

"Yes'm." He brushed his teeth, scowling at himself in the mirror.

Annie checked the tub, and finding it full, turned off the taps. She returned to the sink and filled a glass with water. "Spit," she said to Dallas, "and then rinse."

She held the glass to his lips like she would for a child. "Now strip. It's time for your bath."

He grinned. "I don't strip unless you do."

"Ha-ha. Do you really think you have any power here?" She unbuttoned his shirt, discarded it, pushed him down on the toilet seat, and pulled off his boots and socks. "Now the jeans, Cowboy." She took a deep breath, trying to rein in her scalding desire at the sight of his chest, and unbuckled his belt. She closed her eyes and completed the job. She quivered when, pushing his jeans and boxers to the floor, she brushed the hot skin of his hips.

She opened her eyes slowly. He was completely and totally aroused. With a devil may care grin on his handsome face.

"Damn, Cowboy. You're stinking drunk. How is this possible?"

"Because you're here."

"Whatever. In the tub."

"I'm serious. I'm hard as stone whenever you're around. I can't control it. It's starting to piss me off, to tell you the truth."

"I'll bet. In the tub. Now."

He stepped in obediently. "You gonna wash me?"

"No." She turned.

"Please? At least get in with me. This tub is huge. There's

plenty of room."

"Absolutely not." But she wanted to. So badly she could barely breathe. "I'll go see about your coffee. When I get back here I expect to see your hair washed."

"You promised me kisses if I brushed my teeth."

"I did no such thing."

"You did!"

"Nope. You weren't listening. I said I wouldn't kiss you if you didn't brush your teeth. I didn't say I would if you did."

"That's not fair."

"Too bad. Happy bathing."

She walked out and shut the door behind her. She leaned against the wall, her heart pounding in her chest, imagining the slick warm water flowing over his beautiful body. Panting, she left the room.

Ten minutes later, she ran back in, terrified that he might pass out and drown. What had she been thinking, leaving him alone? He was nearly incapacitated.

"Thank God," she said, when she saw him lounging in the tub, unharmed. But his hair wasn't wet. Now she was pissed. "You were supposed to wash your hair."

"I want you to do it."

"Sorry. No dice."

"Please? I'll stop asking for kisses if you wash my hair."

"You will?"

"No." He chuckled. "But it was worth a try."

"Get cracking. Now."

His lazy smile spread across his face. "No shampoo."

"What? Oh crap." Annie grabbed a bottle of shampoo out of the shower stall and returned to the tub and handed it to him.

Within seconds, he had grabbed her wrist and into the tub she tumbled, fully clothed. She sputtered as water sloshed over the sides of the tub. "Damn you! Now look what you did."

"Now you have to wash my hair."

"I don't *have* to do anything but stay Italian and die, Cowboy." She struggled against his hold. "Let me go!"

"Kiss me."

"No, damn it, let me go!"

For a drunk, his grip on her was like a vise. The more she struggled, the wetter she became, until he eventually turned and pinned her against the side of the tub. She opened her mouth to protest and he clamped onto her, thrusting his tongue between her lips.

The kiss was exquisite torture. She pushed at him at first, but his slick naked body slid under her touch. He, however, fisted his hands in the wet fabric of her blouse and held on for dear life. After several minutes of unsuccessful grappling, she surrendered and sighed into his mouth.

His groans fueled her passion, and she pressed her soggy clothed body to his. When they broke to breathe, he nibbled across her lower lip.

"I want you so much," he said.

"Mmm," was her reply.

"Take off your clothes. Please. Make love with me." His smoky whisper was threaded with desire.

"You're killing me, Dallas. This isn't fair."

"You want me. I can feel it."

"I want you. I won't deny it. I can't. But as soon as you sober up you'll ditch me again. So the answer is no." She pushed him away, successful this time, and scrambled out of the tub. She threw him the bottle of shampoo. "When I come back in here, I expect that hair to be clean, along with the rest of you."

Sopping, she left the bathroom, making a mental note to wipe up the floor before he got out of the tub. In his condition, he'd likely slip and harm himself. She rolled her eyes, berating herself for giving a damn. She'd dry the freaking floor for him. Despite everything, she couldn't bear the thought of him hurting himself.

Back in the bedroom, she stripped off her drenched clothes and pawed through his dresser for something to wear. She found a pair of striped cotton pajamas that looked brand new. She dried herself off and put the garments on. They hung on her, but the pants had a drawstring that she tightened around her waist. She cuffed them to her ankles and looked in the mirror. She laughed to herself, more at the sheer absurdity of her present situation, rather than out of humor. She certainly wouldn't win any fashion contests, but it would do. She picked up her wet clothes and went in search of the dryer.

Traipsing through Dallas's huge house, she finally found the laundry room hidden in a corner of the first floor. Like everything else in the sprawling ranch house, it was oversized, about the size of Annie's living room in her tiny apartment above the clinic. She started her clothes on the gentle cycle, and then went to the kitchen and poured a large mug of coffee for Dallas. She padded barefoot back up the stairs to the bedroom and placed the coffee on Dallas's night table. Sighing, she went into the bathroom to check on him. His hair was wet, though whether it was from a shampoo or their earlier grappling session, she wasn't sure. At any rate, she was done fighting with him, and the water was losing its heat, so she decided it was time to get him to bed.

"Are those my pajamas?" he asked.

"I had to put something on. My clothes are in the dryer."

"God, you look sexy."

"I look like a frumpy housewife."

"You could never look frumpy, Doc. Damn, I want you."

"So you've said." She held out a towel for him. "Come on. Let's dry you off and get you to bed."

"Now you're talkin'."

"For *sleep*, Cowboy. You're going to pass out within minutes."

"Not a chance, as long as I know you're here."

"No problem, then. As soon as I get you bedded down and my clothes are dry, I'm outta here." She jiggled the towel at him. "Come on now."

He let out a sigh and stood up and stepped out of the tub.

"Oops," Annie said. "I meant to wipe up the floor. It's wet, so be real careful, okay?"

"I'm fine. A little chilly, though."

"The water was losing its heat. Don't worry." She rubbed him with the towel. "I've got some hot coffee for you. You'll be snug as a bug in no time."

"Stay with me?"

"Sorry." She wiped the last of the moisture from his body and toweled off his hair. "Come on." She led him into the bedroom and helped him into a clean pair of boxers. "Lie down, now. Like a good boy."

"I am a good boy. I always was. I never made"—he let out a lion's yawn—"the same mistake twice."

"So I've heard." She handed him his coffee. "Take a few sips. It'll warm you."

"Thanks." He took a sip and promptly choked. "Damn.

What is this? Sludge?"

"It's coffee, you idiot. Now drink."

"This ain't coffee, Doc. It's pine tar."

"Quit your whining. I don't drink the stuff. How am I supposed to know how to make it? Now drink."

"Yes'm." He and took two more sips, screwing his face into distortion. "That's all I can take. If your intent was to punish me for my overindulgence, consider yourself successful."

"Funny man. Lie down now."

"Come lie with me."

"Nope."

"Please? I don't want to be alone."

The words crushed into her heart. They were the same words she had said to him the first night they spent together. He had stayed.

So would she.

"All right. I'll bed down in one of your guest rooms."

"No. Here. With me."

"I don't think that's a good idea."

"Don't care. Please."

She sighed. He had stayed with her that first night and held her when she needed him. "Fine. You'll be passed out within ten minutes anyway. Then I can turn the blasted channel to something other than sports."

He chuckled into his pillow. "A romantic comedy I bet."

"Action I think. Something with Bruce Willis or Arnold. Better yet, Gerard Butler. He was hot in *300*."

"Annalisa," he said softly.

"I'm here, Cowboy. Right here." She kissed his forehead lightly.

"I should have never seduced you. Wasn't right."

"Ha. What makes you think *you* did the seducing?" Annie pulled a crisp cotton sheet over his body.

"Shouldn't have. Wasn't gentlemanly." He yawned, his jaw opening farther than Annie thought possible. "I don't do things like that. Never before. But I wanted you so much. Couldn't control myself. Still want you. Annalisa."

"It's okay, Dallas. I understand." She didn't, but he needed comfort right now, not an argument. "Sleep now."

"Annalisa," he said again. "So pretty. Annalisa." He sighed lightly and closed his eyes, his ebony lashes settling against his cheeks. "Annalisa," he whispered. "I love you."

CHAPTER FOURTEEN

Annie sat, mesmerized by his steady slumberous breathing. A lone tear trickled slowly down her cheek. She locked her gaze on his handsome face. The tear fell from her face to his and began meandering through the stubble of several days' growth of beard. She lowered her lips and kissed it away.

He wouldn't remember saying the words, and she wouldn't fool herself into thinking he'd actually meant them. But oh, she wanted to believe it. She so wanted to believe it.

Because she loved him.

She would do what she had to do to be with him. She'd tell him the truth tomorrow. All of it. Every last horrible detail. When he was sober. If he turned his back on her, so be it. She'd be no worse off than she was this very moment.

Forgetting about her desire for an action adventure movie, she clicked off the television, snuggled under the covers, and smoothed her hand over Dallas's shoulder, down his arm, over his hip and thigh. His skin was warming. She cuddled into his back and kissed his shoulder.

"Good night, Cowboy," she whispered.

★ ★ ★

Dallas was still out cold when the sun rose. Annie stretched and got out of bed. She went to the bathroom, took a quick shower, and fetched her clothes from the dryer. Once dressed, she made a tummy-healthy breakfast of scrambled eggs and hash browns, left some for Dallas, and headed in her car to the herding site to check on the sick cattle.

After saying hi to the hands, she examined the stock and breathed a sigh of relief when she found no new sick animals. *It must be the grain then.* She pulled out her cell phone and dialed the clinic to check for messages. Nothing yet. She administered doses of sodium thiosulphate to the recovering steers, but before she could get to her car, Doug Cartwright drove up in his police car with Chad in the passenger seat.

"Hey, Annie," Doug said, the sun casting glints in his red hair. "You're up with the birds."

"Just checking on the stock," she said. "No new sick ones today, which is good."

"That's great," Chad said.

"I tried calling Dallas, but he's not answering," Doug said.

"I'm not surprised." Annie rolled her eyes.

"What do you mean?"

"Nothing. Do you have any news?"

"As a matter of fact, I do. One of my deputies got an anonymous call late last night."

"And?"

"It seems one of Dallas's men may have been paid off to poison the grain."

"I thought he trusted his men."

"He did," Chad said. "But if the price is right, even the most honest man can take a tumble."

Annie knew the truth of Chad's words. She had seen her ex-husband turn from nice guy to violent criminal all for the sake of money. "Any idea which one it is?"

"I'm going to start questioning them today. We'll find the

culprit."

"I hope he hangs," Annie said. "Anyone who hurts innocent animals is a monster."

"Well, babe, hangin' kind of went out a century ago, but we'll see he's taken care of." Doug winked at her.

"You know what I mean."

"I sure do," Chad said, "and I agree with you. Any man who'd hurt an animal ain't nothing but a coward."

"Can't say I disagree with either one of you." Doug raked his fingers through his auburn mane. "I don't want to start questioning the men without Dallas though."

"I can go up to the house and get him," Chad offered.

"If you don't mind, that'd be great," Doug said. "I'll just stay here and keep Annie company."

Annie forced a smile. Doug Cartwright wanted more than to keep her company. It was written all over his face. "No need," she said. "I'm done here."

★ ★ ★

A thousand wildebeests were stampeding inside Dallas's head. It hurt to move. Hell, it hurt to breathe. Fragments of the previous evening came to him. Lying supine on his bed, sucking on a bottle of Macallan. Calling Annie. Annie helping him to the bathroom. Kissing her in the tub. He smiled at that one. Her silky hands helping him into a pair of boxers and putting him to bed. She had stayed. So where was she now?

Cursing, he walked to the bathroom and swallowed four ibuprofen. He quickly dressed and went to the kitchen. On the table was a note.

Good morning, sunshine. Your breakfast is in the fridge.

Microwave for two minutes and eat every bite. I didn't bother making any coffee.

A.

P.S. Some lemongrass herb tea will help the headache.

He smiled. Lemongrass herb tea. *God, she's adorable. God, I love her.* If only she had stayed. If only she were here now. If only...

He was wiping his lips after breakfast when Chad came in the back door. Though his brother shut the door gently, the thud echoed in Dallas's aching head.

"Quiet, will you?"

"Sorry, bro. Doug's out at the site. He needs to talk to you."

"Have you seen Annie?"

"She's out there too, checking on the stock."

"Good. She's still here."

"What? You don't mean—"

"No. Nothing like that. She just...took care of me last night. I had a little too much to drink."

"Sweet girl."

"She is that. I wish..."

"Don't wish, Dallas. Just make it happen."

"Can't. So what does Doug want?"

"He wants to question your men. He got an anonymous call last night that one of them was paid off to poison your stock."

"What? Damn." Dallas rubbed his temples. "I can't believe that."

"I know it's hard to fathom, but it could be true. After all, *someone* poisoned those steers."

"It couldn't have been one of my guys."

"No one else has access to your barns."

"Someone could have broken in."

"But no one did. Doug would have found evidence if there had been a break in."

"God damn it all to hell."

"I hear you talkin'. Trust me, I'm as upset as you are. You should have seen Annie when he told her. She was chomping at the bit for a hanging, no less."

"A hanging?"

"Seems she hates animal abusers."

"Of course she does. She's a vet."

"Yeah, well, she's out there waiting for you."

"She is?"

"Well, Doug is."

"Right." Dallas stood up. "Damn, my head hurts. Let's go."

Annie had left by the time Dallas and Chad got to the herding site.

"Said she had to get back and check in at her office," Doug told them. "Said to call when you found anything out. And she'd call or come out with the lab results when she got them."

"Okay," Dallas said. "Well, let's get on with it."

"This ain't going to be a picnic, Dallas," Doug warned. "Your men'll get defensive."

"Yeah, I know. But let's get it done."

"You're sure you're up to this?"

"Hell, no. I've got twenty jackhammers pounding in my head right now. But damn it, no one messes with my livestock and gets away with it, so let's get it over with."

★ ★ ★

Four hours later, Dallas's head hurt worse than ever. Grilling his men had taken its toll, and Doug had a suspect that he dragged to his station for further questioning. A young man who had been with Dallas for several years. Morgan Bailey. Single. No immediate family in the area. Ripe for the picking.

But young. And weak. A little rough talk from Doug and he had squealed like a pig.

And the worst part? The trail led to a man named Jon Parker, chief legal officer for Beaumont Enterprises, his ex-father-in-law's business.

Jon Parker. Chelsea had mentioned him on more than one occasion. They had been friends since seventh grade or something like that. For a while, Jon had been obsessed with Chelsea. Apparently he still was. But why would Chelsea want to hurt Dallas's cattle? He had given the bitch seven figures, for God's sake.

He pursed his lips and strengthened his resolve. He was more determined than ever never to get involved with a deceptive female again. After last night, he had considered giving Annie another chance.

Wasn't going to happen.

He'd just have to get over her.

Funny, it sounded easy enough, but the thought of it ached in the marrow of his soul.

Speak of the devil. Annie's Beetle drove up the dirt road as Dallas and Chad were waving Doug and the young suspect off.

"Hey, Dr. Annie," Chad said, as she got of her car, "any news?"

"Yeah. Just got the call. Your grasses are clean, like I suspected. But the grain tested positive for cyanide."

"Not a surprise. Doug just took in our suspect."

"Good. You found him already. How are the animals?"

"They're doing well, thanks to you," Chad said.

Dallas still hadn't spoken to Annie. She looked beautiful in a slim denim skirt and a peasant blouse. The sun cast glints in the burgundy highlights of her hair. How he wished things could be different. She turned to him.

"I need to talk to you," she said.

"What about?"

"In private. Please."

"That's my cue," Chad said. "I've got plenty to do. See you all later."

"Can we go up to the house?" Annie asked.

"Uh, sure."

"Good. I'll drive. Hop in."

When they reached the house, Annie headed straight for the kitchen, pulling things from shelves as if she lived there. For a moment, Dallas let himself imagine she did, that this was her house, her kitchen, her home. She looked right in his kitchen. Warmth filled his heart, and he stiffened. He couldn't let the image soften him.

"How's the headache?" she asked, filling a teakettle with water and placing it on a burner.

"Hurts like a bitch."

"I don't doubt it." She pulled two teabags out of her handbag. "Lemongrass," she said, "with some peppermint and linden flowers. The water'll take a minute."

Dallas smiled. He loved the way Annie said "wooder" for water.

"Annie, I should thank you. You know, for last night."

"No problem. I owed you one."

"No. You don't owe me anything."

"Sure I do. That first night, remember? You stayed with me. Comforted me. I owed you the same."

"It was sweet of you."

"Look"—she fidgeted, her fingers shaking as she set a mug on the counter—"I really need to talk to you."

"What about?"

"This is hard for me, Dallas."

"What is it? Are you in trouble?"

"No. Of course not. Nothing like that. I just..." She cleared her throat. "I don't like talking about my first marriage."

"You don't need to."

"Yeah, I think I do." Her voice wavered a little, cracking.

"Your first marriage isn't any of my business."

"I think it is. It's keeping us apart."

"What?"

"I know why you decided not to be with me." Her face turned that adorable shade of pink. "You didn't like that I stayed on the pill when my husband wanted kids. There's a reason, Dallas."

"No." He slammed his fist on the counter, worsening the throbbing in his head. "Damn it. I don't want to hear it."

"What?"

"Annie, I just spent the last four hours interrogating my men. Do you know what I found out? One of them was paid off, probably with my own money. Money I gave Chelsea for a settlement. The whole thing was orchestrated by an employee of Chelsea's father's. She was pissed off about something. Probably got a wild hair up her ass after finding us together."

"An employee. What does that have to do with Chelsea?"

"He's an old friend of hers. Obsessed with her or something."

"Is that any reason for us to be apart?"

"Not the fact that she saw us. Or that some guy is obsessed with her. Of course not. But this morning's whole debacle just reminded me what I had decided when I divorced Chelsea. I have another reason."

"Which is?"

"I won't get involved with another deceptive woman."

"What?"

"You heard me."

"But I'm not a deceptive woman. I'm as honest as they come."

"You deceived your first husband."

"But I had a reason! If you'll just let me explain."

"No. It doesn't matter. What's done is done, and I won't be with you, no matter how much I want it. I won't go through that again. I learned a long time ago—"

"Never to make the same mistake twice." She finished for him, her voice low, robotic.

"Yes. I never make the same mistake twice."

The teakettle whistled on the stove. The shrill singing pounded in Dallas's head.

"Let it steep for three minutes," Annie said, picking up her handbag. "I'm leaving."

"I'm sorry, Annie."

"Don't be."

"Annie—"

"There's nothing for me here," she said.

She walked out of his house. Out of his life.

But she left the knife twisting in his gut. He wondered how long he would suffer before it eased its way out.

★ ★ ★

Fighting back tears, Annie drove to her apartment. She wasn't even all the way unpacked yet, so packing up would be easy. She'd leave tomorrow. Maybe even tonight if she could get a flight. California. That would be a good place to start over. She could even visit Disneyland. The happiest place on earth.

What a crock.

Damn him! Why wouldn't he listen to her? Cocky, stuffy son of a bitch. She'd been ready to pour out her guts to him, to expose herself emotionally to the man she loved. Stupid cowboy.

Were there cowboys in California? No. Surfers and divers, but probably no cowboys. Change would be good. Hopefully she'd make it longer than two weeks there.

Pulling into the alley behind the clinic, she turned off her engine and bowed her forehead against the steering wheel. She let the tears flow, cursing Dallas, cursing Colorado, cursing Logan Riggs. After fifteen minutes, she gulped down her last sob and headed up to her apartment.

Oddly, the door was unlocked again. Had her mother returned? She walked in and gasped at the figure, shadowed in the afternoon sun, sitting on her couch.

"Sweet Annie," Logan Riggs said. "How the hell are you, you conniving bitch?"

CHAPTER FIFTEEN

"What are you doing here? You're in violation of the restraining order I have against you. Not to mention your parole, Riggs."

"Nothing can keep me from the woman I adore." His words dripped with sarcasm. "I thought we could have a little chat."

"I can't imagine what about."

"Well, let's see. It's seems to me, right around the time you had me arrested, your rich childless auntie died, leaving you a healthy little nest egg."

"My rich childless auntie was neither rich nor childless. My share was insubstantial."

"Be that as it may"—he stood, his large frame an imposing presence—"I want my half."

"Half? You mean you're not demanding all of it?"

His thin lips curled into a smirk. "I've always been fair with you, angel. You know you always got what you deserved with me."

Annie rolled her eyes. "Right, Riggs. Sorry to tell you, but the money's gone."

"What do you mean it's gone?"

"Do you understand English? I said it's gone. It wasn't much, and I used it to move here and set up my clinic."

"Well, then, I'll take whatever you have. Give me your pocketbook."

"Are you crazy?"

"I said, give me your pocketbook, bitch." He advanced on her, grabbed her handbag, and pulled out her wallet. "Twenty-five dollars? I came all this way for twenty-five fucking dollars?"

"Hardly worth going back to prison for, was it?"

She didn't see the sucker-punch coming.

"Damn." She rubbed her chin. She should have known better. The thud of pain always came a few seconds afterward. That had always surprised her. She thought she'd feel it right away, but it was always delayed. She licked her lips and tasted the metallic tang of blood.

"We'll just be taking a little trip to the ATM then," Riggs said.

"Small town. No ATM."

"Are you shittin' me?"

"No."

"The bank, then."

"There's nothing there."

"What are you living on?"

"My credit card, what do you think? I've been here two weeks, Riggs. I've done a good business, but my first bills won't even go out until next month."

Riggs grabbed a fistful of her curls and forced her to the couch. "Then I'll take my share out in trade, you stupid whore. I haven't had a good fuck in months." He ripped her blouse open. "You weren't good for much, but damn, you were good for that."

★ ★ ★

"You *what?*" Dusty demanded.

"I told her I didn't want to hear her reasons," Dallas said. "It's not important."

Dusty's small hands clenched into fists. She and Zach had stopped by to check on the cattle, and after Dallas had explained everything, the subject of Dr. Annie had come up.

"You are the most stubborn idiot on this planet," Dusty said, seething. "You have no idea what you've done. Do you know what that woman has been through?"

"It doesn't matter," Dallas said calmly. "I never make the same mistake twice."

"Punch him," Dusty said to Zach. "Whoop his ass good. He deserves it."

"Simmer down, darlin'," Zach said. "God knows I've wanted to whoop his ass on many occasions, and I'll be happy to oblige later, but first I need to know what the hell is going on."

"You're as bad as he is. Neither one of you understands anything!" Dusty paced the floor, her rosy cheeks turning bright red. "You grew up here, in luxury, with enough money to buy whatever you wanted. Two loving parents, never any problems. Well, this isn't the real world. The real world has pain, and fear, and sadness, and sickness, and things that just aren't fair!"

"Dusty—"

"No, Zach. I won't calm down. Your brother just let a woman walk out of his life because he's a short-sighted, pompous moron who claims to be a gentleman. Well, Dallas, a gentleman would have listened to his lady. You're a fool."

Dallas breathed steadily. His shattered heart ached in his chest, but he forced his voice to remain steady. "I had good reason for letting her go, Dusty."

"Do you love her?"

"That's not your concern."

"Damn it, Dallas. Do you love her?"

He swallowed. Why lie? "Yes."

"Oh!" Dusty rammed her fisted hands into Dallas's chest. "You make me so damn mad! You have no idea what she's been through, why she made the decisions she made."

"And you do?"

"Yes. She told me everything. She cried in my arms, the poor thing. And you tossed her out like garbage. I hope you spend the rest of your life alone, Dallas McCray. It's better than you deserve."

"Dusty," Zach said, pulling his wife away from his brother. "What did Annie tell you?"

"I won't break her confidence."

"You don't have to tell me," he said, "but don't you think you should tell Dallas?"

"No, I don't. He doesn't care, and I gave Annie my word."

"She tried to tell me this afternoon," Dallas said. "I wouldn't listen."

"You're a fool."

"Maybe I am. Was it bad?"

"Was it bad? You really haven't got a clue, do you? Do you think every woman is like Chelsea? Deceptive and shallow?"

"Damn it, Dusty, answer me. Was it bad?"

"It was the worst, and I've got news for you. I would have done the same thing in her shoes. Maybe even worse, come to think of it." Two tears streamed down Dusty's crimson cheeks. "Sometimes life deals you a rotten hand, and you find yourself willing to do things you never thought you'd do to get out of it." She sniffed and took the red bandana Zach offered her. "When I got sick, I remember thinking I'd do anything to be well. I mean anything. Deceptive. Illegal. I didn't care. I would have sold my soul to the devil himself if it would have made me well again." She wiped her eyes. "Neither of you will ever understand that because you've both had silver spoons in your mouths your whole lives!"

"Her marriage was bad, huh?" Zach said.

"Yes. Of course it was. I can tell you that much. It was worse than bad."

"Then why did she stay in it?"

"Probably for the same reason Dallas stayed with Chelsea for ten years. She didn't want to fail at what was supposed to be the most important relationship of her life." She turned her angry eyes on Dallas. "You're more alike than you think you are, you and Annie. You two were a match made in heaven, and you threw her away."

"God," Dallas said, his stomach knotting. "He hurt her, didn't he?"

Dusty nodded. "I won't say any more than that. I can't believe this never occurred to you."

Visions of Annie's beautiful body lying battered tormented Dallas's mind. His body trembled and his stomach lurched. For a moment, he thought he was going to be sick. "I don't understand how a man could hurt a woman. His wife. A cowboy wouldn't. A gentleman wouldn't."

"God, you two have been so sheltered!" Dusty ranted. "You make me sick! Not all men are gentlemen, Dallas. And I hate to break it to you, not all cowboys are either. You know this. You're not stupid."

"She seems so together. So strong." Dallas shook his head. "Like she hasn't had any bad stuff in her life." How could he have been so wrong?

"What do you want her to do? Sit around wallowing in self-pity? Where would I be if I had done that?"

"Damn," Dallas said. "Damn."

"You should have let her explain. She's not Chelsea, Dallas. She's Annie. She's sweet, and kind, and smart, and wonderful. She has so much to give, and she wanted to give it to you. And you sent her away."

"Shit." Dallas plunked down in a chair and cupping his head in his hands. "What have I done?"

"Sounds like you've fucked up, brother," Zach said. "Royally. Course it's not the first time."

"Can it, Zach, and help me figure out what to do."

"Damn, you *are* dense. Go after her, for God's sake."

"Right. Go after her. I'll go after her. Oh my God, what if she won't have me?" The fear of it sank into his heart like a rusty blade.

"I wouldn't blame her if she didn't," Dusty said, "after the way you've treated her."

"Neither would I," Dallas admitted. "She's got to listen to me. She's just got to." He picked up his cell phone and dialed her number. No response. "That's odd," he said. "She always picks up her cell. She never wants to miss a sick animal."

"The battery's probably dead. Besides, you should see her in person," Zach said. "Groveling is much more effective that way."

"Yeah. Yeah." Dallas whistled for Jet. "You're coming with me, Buddy. She's a sucker for you." He gave his dog a pat on the head. "I'm going to need all the help I can get."

★ ★ ★

Riggs hadn't raped her. He hadn't been able to get an erection, thank God. Instead, he had beaten her. She drifted in and out of consciousness in the backseat of a moving car. Every muscle in her body ached, but at least she hadn't had to have sex with him. He had punished her for it, but she'd rather have the pain than the humiliation of knowing he'd violated her sexually. Now, tied and gagged, she had no idea where she was going.

He would kill her. Of that she was certain. The beating hadn't been bad, come to think of it. She'd suffered much worse in the past. When she fought back. Today, she hadn't had the strength or the desire to fight back. Funny. If she'd lain like a dead fish that last time, she probably wouldn't have spent so much time in the hospital.

Yes, he would kill her. He had violated his parole and he had battered her. He couldn't afford to leave any witnesses alive. No one would look for her. Dallas had sent her away. No one would even know she was gone until the next person walked into the clinic with an animal. Even then, in a small town, people would think she had just closed up for a little while.

There was really no hope.

Her life would end, and no one would know.

Or give a damn.

CHAPTER SIXTEEN

Annie wasn't in the clinic, so Dallas walked to the back of the building and went up to her apartment. When she didn't answer his knock, he tried the door, surprised to find it open. "Well, Buddy," he said to Jet, "we'll just go on in and wait for her. Maybe we can make her a pot of herb tea."

Dallas entered the apartment, Jet at his heels. He looked around. Nothing seemed amiss, but the knife in his gut told him something wasn't right. He gazed over the living area, looking for something, anything, out of place.

He found it. Her cell phone. It lay on the couch, partially buried underneath a cushion. Annie never went anywhere without her phone. He picked it up and looked around. There, thrown in a corner, was her handbag. Dallas dug through it. He found her wallet, but it contained no cash or credit cards.

His bowels clenched as worry and fear poured into him. Something had happened to her. He quickly dialed Dusty.

"Hello?"

"Dusty, it's Dallas. I'm at Annie's. She's not here, but her cell phone and purse are. I'm afraid something has happened to her. Please. I know you gave her your word, but I need to know anything she told you that might help me figure out where to find her."

"Oh God, Dallas."

"What? Tell me!"

"Her ex-husband. He was in prison for what he did to her,

but he was released a few days ago. On parole."

His heart thumped. "Fuck. Anything else?"

"Just that you'd better find her. And fast. I'll call Zach and Chad. You call Doug. We need the authorities on this."

"Yeah. Yeah." Dallas raked his hands through his hair, his nerves tightening. Knots turned and twisted in his stomach. Damn, he was going to be ill. He swallowed and willed away the nausea. *Annie. Concentrate on Annie.*

Once he had called Doug, he went into Annie's bedroom. She had unpacked several more boxes since he had been there last. Particularly interesting was her veterinary doctorate. *Annalisa DeSimone Riggs.*

Her married name.

He shot back into the living room and picked up her cell phone. Not much battery left, but enough to check her contacts. Ma and Pop. Lillian. Macy. Drew. None of the names rang a bell. She had friends he didn't even know about. He barely knew the woman he loved. But he'd get to know her. He'd get her back and learn everything about her, and accept and love every single detail, no matter what it was.

He continued flipping through the list. *Riggs.* There it was. No first name. Could it really be that easy? He dialed the number. It rang several times before clicking into voice mail. "This is Riggs. You know what do."

Dallas clicked off the phone and dialed the number again.

"Yeah?" An exasperated low voice growled.

"Riggs."

"Yeah? What is it?"

"I need to speak to Annie."

A pause. Then, "Who the fuck is this?"

"Is she okay?"

"You tell me who the fuck you are, asshole."

"A friend of hers. Please. I need to know if she's all right."

"What makes you think I have her?"

"Give me a little credit. You don't want to go back to prison, do you?"

"This conversation is over, pal."

"No! Please, don't hang up. I... I have money. I'll give you whatever you want. Plane tickets. A car. Whatever. Just please don't hurt her."

"You must think I'm some kind of moron. How do I know you're on the level?"

"You don't. But the cops are after you. They'll find you eventually. I don't care about finding you. All I care about is Annie. Please."

"I need a hundred thou. Cash. And a new car. Untraceable. Can you handle that?"

"Not until I know Annie's safe."

"She's fine. She's in the backseat of my car. Out cold."

Dallas's gut clenched. The son of a bitch had hurt her. This was not going to end well for him. He took a deep breath. He had to keep his cool for her. "I want to talk to her."

"I told you, she's out cold."

"Pull over and wake her up. Until you can prove you have her and she's okay, you get nothing from me."

"Christ. Fine. Give me a few minutes."

Dallas's heart raced, and he prayed the line would hold. God only knew where Riggs and Annie were. They could drive out of cell phone range at any time.

After several minutes of agony, Dallas finally heard her voice. "Hello?"

It was her. He'd know that sweet husky Jersey accent

anywhere. His heart leaped. "Annie. Oh God, Annie. It's me. Dallas. I love you. I love you, Doc. Are you all right?"

"Touching," Riggs said. "But she didn't hear any of it. I took the phone from her as soon as she said hello."

"You fucking son of a bitch!"

"Don't get testy with me, boy. I have something you want, obviously. Who'd have thought the little bitch would rope another sucker into loving her?" Riggs laughed eerily. "I see she's worth much more than I imagined. But I'm not one to be greedy. I believe the price was a hundred K and a car."

"Done. Where can I pick up Annie?"

"I've done time, friend. I'm not stupid. You bring the car and the cash to me. Make sure the tank is full."

"Fine. Name the place. You're holding all the cards here, Riggs. All I want is Annie. But"—he forced the next words out between clenched teeth—"if you so much as touch another hair on her head, the deal is off."

"Don't worry. She'll be good as new within a day or two. She always had spirit, that one. Bounced right back. Never could break her. The bitch."

The anger jolted into Dallas like red heat. How dare he talk about Annie like that? *Damn it, Dallas. Stay focused.* "Just give me the drop off point, Riggs. I'll bring the car and the cash."

"I'm on Highway thirty-seven. Just crossed the New Mexico border. There's a town called Foghorn a few miles away. I'll stop there. You call this number when you get there. And friend?"

I'm not your friend, asshole. "What?"

"You call the cops, and the deal's off."

"Understood." Dallas flipped the phone shut. He wished

he hadn't called Doug. Should he stay here and wait for the sheriff to arrive, or should he leave for Foghorn?

Leave for Foghorn. He'd get to Annie. The cops would just spook Riggs.

Annie. God, Annie. How he loved her.

When he and Jet were in the car, he gunned the engine and headed back toward his home. He ran into the house and into his study, quickly opening the safe on the wall behind the portrait of his parents. He counted out $100,000 in bills, placed them in a briefcase, and grabbed something else out of his safe.

His sharpshooter pistol. He called it Jake.

Dallas McCray was a champion marksman, and he had no intention of letting Riggs get away.

★ ★ ★

Had she talked to someone on the phone? Annie twisted through the haze in her mind, trying to make sense of what had happened. Riggs had held the phone to her ear. Just as quickly, it was gone. She had said hello. Hadn't she?

Didn't matter anyway. Riggs had replaced her gag, and now she lay across the backseat of the car, jostling uncomfortably with each bump in what must be a dirt road.

How? How had it come to this?

Logan Riggs had been a kind man once. A handsome, kind man who had swept Annie off her feet.

She opened one eye and then the other. As the cloudiness subsided, the blur that was Riggs faded slowly into focus. *Odd.* Same tawny hair and light brown eyes. Same long nose and full mouth. Same neck corded with muscle. He was still handsome. Nearly as handsome as when he had first swept her off her feet nine years before, during her first year of vet school. He had dreams then. Or so he had said. Dreams of making it big in the casino industry. He had worked his way up into mid-level management of one of the biggest hotel and casino companies in Atlantic City. Annie had married him the summer before her last year of vet school, and they had been happy for a little while.

But then the gambling.

And after that, the drinking.

The gambling debts made him angry, unnerved, and the drink took that angry nervousness and turned it into violence. Violence directed toward her.

At first it was only the occasional slap. Then the tearful apology. When she suffered a miscarriage, he blamed her. After her D and C, her stomach cramping from the procedure, he had punched her in the gut. The next day she called her doctor and went back on the pill.

A rational decision. Of course, the better decision would have been to leave Riggs. Over and over she had berated herself for letting it go on as long as it had. She had fallen out of love with him. He had hurt her. He had stolen from her. Yet still she had stayed. For more abuse. Things would get better, he told her. I love you, he told her. I'm so sorry. Over and over again. He was sorry.

Annie closed her eyes, squeezing them shut as hard as she could, trying to block out the memories that came blazing back from the deep recesses of her mind.

Like a curtain parting, revealing the final act of a play.

★ ★ ★

On the third anniversary of her marriage to Logan Riggs, Annie sat on her couch with a mug of chamomile tea, looking through her wedding album. Riggs had been happy that day. His eyes shone with dedication, with love. He had cut his unruly tawny hair at Annie's mother's request. It lay cropped above his ears, his small diamond ear stud visible even in the smaller pictures. Annie had loved the diamond stud. Clad in a basic black tuxedo, he looked as though he had stepped out of the pages of GQ Magazine.

Annie wore an ivory sheath. Her mother had warned her against white. It would make Annie's pale skin look washed out, Sylvia had said. So ivory it was, with a beaded sweetheart neckline and a slim skirt that accentuated Annie's curves. Her long dark hair was swept off her neck into an elaborate cascade of curls falling down her bare back. Riggs had caressed her back during their first dance as man and wife, his fingers as gentle as a dove's wings feathering across her white skin. During their photography session at the reception, when he stood behind her, he had moved her hair to the side and brushed his lips over her neck and shoulders.

Yes, he had loved her. Part of her believed he still did. He said it often enough. Yet, if he truly loved her, why did he let himself lose control? He hadn't hurt her badly. Never any real damage. But why?

The timer on the oven snapped her out of her wedding daydream. Her Osso Bucco. An anniversary treat for Riggs. For the last several weeks, he had been calm and devoted. Calling when he would be late. Treading softly when he came in so he wouldn't wake her. Thanking her for her work around the house. Asking about the animals she treated. An effort. He was making an effort.

She would reward him with a gourmet Italian feast. Osso Bucco. Risotto Calabrese. Focaccia with three cheeses. Artichoke and fennel salad. And for dessert, her mother's creamy cannolis. She smiled, thinking about the cannolis. Riggs had never once asked her to make Tiramisu. She loved him for that.

The robust aroma of garlic and veal wafted out of the oven as Annie set the meat on a trivet and covered it with foil to rest. She turned on the burner under the pan of risotto and went to work on her salad. She was slicing a bulb of fennel when she heard the garage door open. She smiled. Riggs might not be the perfect husband, but he did love her cooking. Although he had voiced his share of complaints during their short marriage, he had never once criticized any of her meals.

He entered the kitchen from the garage, and Annie, still smiling, looked up at him.

Uh-oh. Something had gone wrong. His pursed lips formed a line below his nose, and his ears were red.

When Riggs was angry, his ears always turned red.

Annie put down the fennel and wiped her hand. "Happy anniversary," she said and held out her arms.

"What's so fucking happy about it? Two years of being saddled with you?"

Annie breathed deeply, trying not to let his words hurt her. "Three years, actually."

"God. It's been three? I'm a glutton for punishment. What's that awful smell?"

"What smell?"

"Veal. It's veal. Christ, I hate veal."

"You don't hate veal. I just made veal piccata last week and you ate two help—"

Slap. Right across the face. A few minutes of numbness, and then stinging pain. Annie didn't fall.

"Jesus, Riggs. It's our anniversary." She willed herself not to cry, but her eyes misted anyway.

"If say I hate veal, I hate veal, you stupid tramp."

"But I made a special dinner for our anniversary. Osso Bucco. It's my mother's recipe."

"Why would I want to eat anything your bitch mother serves, huh?" He slammed his fist onto the counter.

Annie backed away. "What happened today? Why are you so upset?"

"Like you care."

"Of course I care. I'm your wife."

"True." He looked at her lasciviously. "I think I'll take some conjugal rights. Now." He grabbed her wrist and pulled her into his body, knocking the wind out of her lungs. He slammed his mouth onto her and bit her, drawing blood.

She pushed at him, but he was too strong. "Riggs," she said, when he lifted his head to breathe. "Not like this. Please. Let's have our celebration dinner. We can...talk. You can tell me what's wrong. I want to help."

"Talk? Talk? I want to fuck." He pushed her to the floor. "But I can't fuck with this disgusting smell in here!" He grabbed the glass pan of Osso Busco from the counter. "It's hot, goddamnit!" He threw the pan at Annie's face.

"Auugghhh!" she cried. The heavy hardness of the glass knocked into her forehead and fell to her chest, and the hot meat seared her eyelids and cheeks.

Scarred. Her face would be scarred. She had never been

vain, but the thought of losing her beauty at her husband's hand was too much to bear. The heat of anger flowed into her veins. She grabbed the glass pan, as yet unbroken, and stood up, her head woozy. She rushed at him, forced her arms from her body with as much energy as she could muster, and hit Riggs on the head with the glass pan.

It shattered, knocking him back a few steps. A red trickle of blood oozed down his cheek where a shard of glass cut him.

"Bitch," he seethed through clenched teeth. "You won't get away with that." He grabbed her long hair, forced her to the kitchen floor, and rubbed her face in the ruined Osso Bucco. "Why don't you eat the rancid meat, you whore! Eat it, while I fuck you until you can't move!"

Annie struggled to breathe, congealed meat juices forcing their way into her nose. She snorted and coughed as he continued to smear her face into the greasy mess.

"Bitch. Stupid fucking bitch. Clean up this fucking mess!"

He thunked her head into the floor. She must have blacked out for a few seconds, because the next thing she knew he was on his feet, kicking her in the side.

She screamed and curled into a fetal position to escape his pelting blows. While her body took the abuse, she reached across the floor looking for something, anything, to use as a weapon. She found the leg of the kitchen table and grabbed onto it. She tried to get a footing to pull herself up, but the floor was slimy from the Osso Bucco.

Her Osso Bucco. Her masterpiece. Her anniversary treat for her husband.

Her husband who was beating her senseless.

The dull aches turned into sharp pain as Riggs continued to kick her. He yelled, but she no longer understood the words.

A searing pain shot from her right elbow up to her shoulder, ending in a torturous agony so intense she blacked out again. Several seconds later she awakened. Riggs had stopped kicking her and was forcing her skirt around her waist. He ripped off her panties. Her left hand still gripped the table leg, so she willed her right hand to reach for something. Anything.

But it wouldn't move. The acute pain throbbed. She couldn't move her arm. Damn, she couldn't move her arm!

Although the table leg served no purpose, she held onto it as a sort of buoy. For some odd reason that she couldn't rationalize, the thought of letting go tormented her. But she had to. Her other arm wasn't working. Bracing herself, she uncurled her fingers from around the wooden pole and began groping for a makeshift weapon.

Nothing. There was nothing.

She writhed, engulfed in heated pain but determined to get away. The breeze from the ceiling fan flowed over her bare buttocks. Then clammy hands, Riggs's firm pinching hold.

"Spread your legs, bitch." He wrenched her thighs apart and plastered himself between them. The slow unzipping of his fly went straight to her stomach. She threw up.

"So I make you sick, do I? Well, you make me just as sick. More so, even. I can't stand the sight of you."

"Then why do you want to fuck me?" she croaked out. "If you can't stand—"

"Shut up!" He kneed her between the legs.

Her mind had gone numb. That was the only reason for her next reaction. She laughed. She erupted in gales of giggles. "You're so stupid, Riggs," she said, her voice a cracking whisper. "That doesn't work on girls."

"Don't you ever fucking call me stupid!" He thrust his

fingers into her with such force her head propelled forward and slammed into the table leg that had been her anchor. She groaned as tiny sparks of light danced in her eyes.

"How do you like that, bitch?" Riggs continued to violate her with his hands. "Nice, huh?"

His fingers stretched her dry sex, shooting pain into her chest. God, let him just get it over with, she pleaded to herself. I tried. I tried to get away. I've done all I can. Just let it be over.

He removed his fingers and thrust into her with his hard cock. She heaved again, but threw up only yellow stomach acid. With each thrust, her head slammed into the table leg until she finally lost consciousness.

The blackness was a welcome relief.

★ ★ ★

When she awoke later, she'd had no idea how much time had passed. For a few moments she'd had the sensation of being outside her body, suspended against the ceiling. Then she had slammed back into her body with full force, and the torturous suffering began. Her right arm lay limply on the floor. It throbbed, and she still couldn't move it. Wetness trickled out of her private parts and she gagged, remembering the rape. Her cheeks and eyes still stung from the burns, and her body ached all over from the kicking.

She had crawled, with only one arm, to the phone and dialed 9-1-1.

Then she had gone to the hospital, and Riggs had gone to prison.

The meat hadn't been hot enough to do any lasting damage, despite the fact it had felt like hot coals raking her face at the time. But her right shoulder had been dislocated, and her left kidney had been bruised. The doctors had been amazed that no bones were broken. Still more skin than not was black–and-blue.

Two weeks later, she had been released.

She had rebuilt her life over the next two years. She took self-defense classes. Got counseling. Scrimped and saved. Then her aunt had died, leaving her a small inheritance. With money in the bank, she made her move. A small rural town in south eastern Colorado was looking for a vet.

Three hundred days of sunshine a year...

For two weeks, she had lived in Bakersville, tending to animals, making friends, finding love. Or what she had foolishly thought was love.

And now her past was back to haunt her. Riggs out on parole. Dallas, the cowboy she loved, had left her. All because of a decision she had made to protect an innocent child from her violent ex-husband.

She turned her head into the vinyl car seat and let the fog take her brain once more.

CHAPTER SEVENTEEN

FUBAR, as Granddaddy Dallas used to say. Fucked up beyond all recognition.

During the two plus hours it took for Dallas to get to Foghorn, all he could think about how he had fucked up this situation beyond all recognition.

God. Annie. He'd make it up to her. He'd get to her in time. He had to.

His cell phone vibrated and he picked it up.

"Dallas? Doug Cartwright. Where the hell are you?"

"I'm on my way to Annie, Doug."

"Damn it. What the hell are you trying to pull?"

"I know where she is, and I'm going to get her. Don't try to stop me. I love her."

"If you love her, then... What? You *love* her?"

"Yes. I love her, I love her, I love her. Her ex-husband, Riggs, is waiting for me in Foghorn. I'm taking him a hundred K in cash and I'll give him my truck. I'll bring Annie back in his car."

"Dallas, this is not the most intelligent thing you've ever done. Come back here and let us take care of it. I'll have the state patrol there in—"

"No! No cops, Doug." Dallas's heart nearly stopped. "Please. He'll hurt her. He's a loose cannon. He's violated parole and he's beaten her again. I can't take the chance he'll harm her."

"Dallas, don't be a fool."

"The only foolish thing I ever did was let that lady walk away from me. I love her, and I'll bring her back. Just give me two hours, Doug. That's all I ask."

"I can't do it. I have a job to do."

"Please. Please. As a friend. I'm asking as a friend."

Doug's harsh breath permeated the other side of the line. "You're putting me in an awkward position, Dallas. I don't want that lady in any more danger than she already is. There are professionals who can handle this."

"Please. Just two hours. That's all I'm asking."

"All right. I hope to God I don't regret this."

"You won't. I'll bring her home. I promise."

"Don't do anything stupid."

Dallas eyed his sharpshooter on the passenger seat. "I won't." He clicked the call off.

"Well, fella," he said to Jet, "let's bring our Annie home."

He gunned across the border into New Mexico.

★ ★ ★

"Motherfucker better show up."

Annie heard Riggs's voice and felt his arms shaking her.

"Wake up, bitch. Come on."

The thickness lifted.

Riggs. Riggs was here. Annie's thoughts came in splintered fragments. Dallas. The pill.

Right. The pill.

Going on the pill had been the right decision. No matter what Dallas thought. If he had let her explain, he no doubt would have understood. But he didn't love her. At least not enough to trust that she'd had a valid reason for her lying to her husband.

Riggs nudged her again. "You're in luck, sweet Annie. It seems you have an admirer who's willing to pay good money for your return. Let's not disappoint him. Or me."

The throbbing inside Annie's head felt like a machine gun. Admirer? Good money? Riggs was obviously delusional. No one would give money for her return. No one even knew she was gone.

The buzz of Riggs's cell phone hammered in her ear.

"Riggs," he said.

Annie strained, feeling every synapse of her brain firing, trying to understand his words and make sense of them.

"I'm at the second exit..." Riggs's voice trailed off. Then, "Abandoned shed...money...no cops."

He clicked his cell phone shut. "Now we wait."

Dallas's stomach gnawed at him as he exited the highway in the small ghost town of Foghorn, New Mexico. He drove along the desolate dirt road until he saw the abandoned wooden shed to the east. Turning, he noticed a car parked behind the shed, invisible from the road. He pulled his pickup over and stopped. "You need to stay here, fella," he said to Jet. Dallas carefully took his loaded sharpshooter out of its case and tucked it in the back of his waistband. "You won't fail me, will you, Jake?" He pulled his T-shirt over the gun and grabbed the suitcase full of bills. "Wish me luck, boy." He gave Jet a quick pet on the head. "I'm coming, Annie," he said through clenched teeth. "I'm coming, baby. He'll never hurt you again."

He exited the vehicle, leaving the windows open slightly for his dog. He dialed Riggs once more. "I'm here," was all he said.

"No tricks," the irrational voice said into his ear. "Bring the money behind the shed, to the car."

"I want to see her first."

"I'll have her. You just keep your part of the deal."

"You hurt her and the deal's off."

"Funny man. Who's holding the cards here? Just get back here. Don't come more than a hundred feet. You lay down the cash when you see me."

"Understood."

He walked toward the shed, and then gasped when he saw the man holding Annie's limp body, a knife to her throat.

"Christ, what have you done to her?"

"Don't come any closer. The cash, please."

Annie's cheeks were tear-stained and her eyes sunken. She had a glassy look about her, as though she wasn't sure what was happening. He had beaten her. The bastard would pay.

Dallas held out the cash, buying himself some time. Riggs held Annie to his left, attempting to use her as a shield. But he wasn't the brightest bulb. He left several areas wide open. Dallas surveyed each possible entry point quickly. A few might graze Annie, and he wouldn't risk hurting her.

But Riggs's right calf was wide open. Perfect. He'd be disabled but not seriously injured.

Dallas slowly laid the suitcase full of cash on the ground.

"Now back away," Riggs said.

"Not without her."

"You'll get her when I get the cash."

"Have it your way," Dallas said.

Within another few seconds, Riggs thrashed on the ground, Dallas's bullet in his shin.

"You motherfucker! We had a deal."

Dallas ignored the cursing and went to Annie, who had fallen with Riggs. Her battered cheek lay against the hard dirt. He lifted her in his arms, carried her to his pickup, and laid her on the wide backseat. "Go on, boy," he said to Jet, "let me see to her."

He pushed her hair out of her eyes and covered her face with kisses. "Oh, Annie. Baby. My love. I'm so sorry. I'm so, so sorry." He kissed her lips gently and pulled her to his chest, cradling her. "I'm so sorry," he said into her hair. "No one will ever hurt you again. I swear it. Not as long as I live, my love."

"D-Dallas?"

"Annie!" Dallas stopped himself from jumping, not wanting to disturb her weak body. His heart hammered against his sternum. "Thank God you're all right."

"Where am I?"

"You're in my truck. Riggs is... He's... Well, he's been shot."

"Who shot him?"

"I did."

"What? You, Cowboy?"

"I'm a crack shot, remember?" He gazed into her violet eyes. They looked tired. Worn.

"How did you find me?"

"I'll always find you. I'll never let you go again. I'm so sorry, Annie. I love you. I love you so much."

"You...love me?"

"With all my heart."

"But what about—"

"I was an idiot. A moron. A complete fool. Forgive me?

Please?"

"But—"

"Annie, please. I don't know what I'll do if you don't."

"But you—"

A knock on the car window jolted them both. Riggs stood there, a pistol pointing at them.

"Oh God, Dallas."

"Don't worry, Doc. I'll take care of this."

"But he's got a gun."

"Yeah. But he's injured. He can barely stand, and I'd be willing to bet I'm a better shot."

"But—"

"I'll never fail you again, Annie. I promise."

He kissed her head and opened the car door with a yank, knocking Riggs to the ground. Dallas leaped upon him, tossing his gun aside and pummeling him with his fists.

"How dare you hurt the woman I love?" he yelled. "You sorry son of a bitch." His fist thudded into Riggs's jaw. Blood poured from Riggs's nose. Dallas wrung his hands around Riggs's neck and forced his head into the dirt. "You son of a bitch. Son of a whore." Thump. "Goddamned bastard!" Thump. Thump. Thump. Riggs's eyes rolled into the back of his head.

"Dallas!"

It was Annie.

"Stay in the truck, Annie." Dallas continued to beat the man, long after he had lost consciousness. It felt too good to stop. Too damn good.

"Dallas, listen to me."

"I'll take care of this." *Thump. Thump. Thump.*

"But you'll kill him!"

The words jarred him. He looked at his fingers around the man's throat, the blood gushing from his nose, his battered face, his wounded leg. Kill him? The man deserved far worse. But Dallas wouldn't spend the rest of his life in prison for this sorry excuse for a human being. He had very nearly lost control. Thank God for Annie.

He left Riggs's body slumped on the ground, pulled out his cell phone, and dialed 9-1-1. After explaining the situation, he returned to Annie.

"I'm sorry you had to see that."

"Are you kidding?" She pulled him to her. "I loved seeing that. I just didn't want to turn you into something you'd regret."

"Thank you." He kissed the top of her head. "I love you."

"Yeah. You said that. But—"

"But what?" His heart lurched. He had come for her. He had saved her. What could possibly go wrong?

"I'm not sure I can be with you. Not after everything. I... I don't ever want to experience that kind of hurt again, Dallas."

"I'll never hurt you."

"You don't understand." Annie blinked.

Was she having trouble seeing? She coughed a little, and he held her close and rubbed her back as she gasped. He spoke what he hoped were soothing words into her ear and silently thanked God he could hold her. The woman he loved.

After several deep breaths, she spoke again. "All of Riggs's beatings. All of his vicious and vile words. His—" She choked out a sob. "He went to prison for beating and raping me."

"I know, baby. I'm so sorry."

"No. I-I'm not asking for pity. I'm trying to...that is...what I'm trying to say is that, all the times he hurt me, well, they hurt. Badly. But I'd gladly go through it all again to save myself from the cutting pain of you rejecting me."

"I'm not rejecting you."

"But you did. You wouldn't let me explain."

"I was a fool. I don't deserve your forgiveness. But I love you, Annie. More than I ever thought I could love another person. I don't want to live without you."

"If..." She sighed. "Dallas. If you hadn't rejected me, I wouldn't have gone home and found Riggs waiting, and I wouldn't have..."

Had someone shot him? In the heart?

"Oh God." Dallas raked his fingers through his thick hair. She wasn't going to forgive him. She blamed him for this current situation. A knife slashed through him, past the ache in his heart all the way into his marrow.

She was right.

"Please, Annie."

"I can't, Dallas. I just can't."

"Do you feel anything for me?"

"Yes."

"Then..." But he couldn't finish.

She pulled away from him, and he realized he was neglecting her well-being. "We'll talk about this later," he said. "Right now you need medical attention."

Her body slumped back into the seat. "I'm fine. Just exhausted. I've been through...worse."

He didn't doubt it, and the thought cut into him like a dagger. Why hadn't he protected her? Why had he let her go? He sent Jet into the backseat with her.

"Hey, cutie," she said to the dog. "I've missed you."

But she hadn't missed *him*, Dallas thought to himself. He had blown it. Big time.

Yep. FUBAR.

Pushing his pain to the back of his mind, he concentrated on Annie. He drove as fast as he could to the nearest hospital and took her into the emergency room. The local police came soon after and bombarded him with questions. His head throbbed from the interrogation.

Much later, in the early hours of the morning, when Annie had been bandaged and pronounced fit to leave, he led her to his truck. "Come on, Doc. Let's get you home."

He peeked in the rearview mirror. Annie dozed fitfully, her arms encircled around Jet's soft body, as Dallas drove back to Bakersville.

He had learned a long time ago that crying was a waste of time.

He cried anyway.

CHAPTER EIGHTEEN

"Are you sure you want to do this?"

Annie clicked her suitcase shut and turned around to face Dusty. After three days of broth and TLC from her friend, Annie was as good as new except for a few bruises. Riggs hadn't beaten her nearly as badly as she'd feared. It had seemed worse at the time because it had been so long. She bounced back quickly.

"I can't stay, Dusty."

"We need you here."

"You'll find another vet."

"But not another Annie."

Annie smiled and hugged her friend. "We'll e-mail."

"It's not the same." Dusty sat down on Annie's bed and began to sort through a box of books. "He's hurting."

Annie sighed. "So am I."

"But this is silly. Neither one of you needs to be hurting."

"He hasn't come by."

"He thinks you hate him."

"I don't hate him." *God no, I don't hate him.*

"He loves you."

"He told me."

"Do you love him?"

"It doesn't make a difference."

"How can you say that? Of course it does!"

"No. It really doesn't. He abandoned me when I needed

him. He cast me aside and wouldn't let me explain myself. What kind of love is that? What kind of trust is that? I won't get back into that kind of marriage."

Dusty chuckled.

"What is so funny?"

"You sound just like him. That's why he wouldn't let you explain in the first place. He was afraid of getting into another marriage like his first. Now you're saying the same thing."

Annie sat down on her bed, exasperated. There was truth in Dusty's words. "He hasn't tried to contact me."

"Can you blame him?"

"No."

"Come home with me. Have dinner with Zach and Sean and me. Maybe we can convince you to stay."

"Dusty, if he hadn't sent me away, maybe I wouldn't have gone home and found Riggs waiting."

"And maybe you would have."

"Maybe I would have, but I would have fought back like I used to. I... I'm embarrassed to say I just let him beat me. I didn't think there was anything to live for. The man I loved had just—"

"Ah-ha!"

"What?"

"You love him."

"So what?"

"You will not walk away from love, Annie DeSimone. I won't let you."

"It's not your decision."

"You're right." Dusty rose from the bed. "But as your friend, I plan to use everything within my power to convince you to stay. To not give up on love. Follow me."

"Where are we going?"

"Oh, just to the living room. I think I heard the doorbell."

"What the hell are you talking about? There was no doorbell."

"Didn't you hear it?"

"Of course not."

"Gee. I'm almost sure I did. You'd better check."

"*You'd* better check. Your ears, that is."

"Humor me. I know I heard it."

"Fine. God." Annie walked to the door and opened it. Sitting on the welcome mat, his tail thumping happily, was Jet. "What in the world?" Annie knelt down to pet him. Around his neck was an envelope tied to a string. "How long have you been sitting here, cutie?" Annie detached the envelope and opened it. Something fell out and clinked on the cement. Annie paid no attention and unfolded the note.

Jet and I love you and miss you, Annie. If you give me another chance, I swear you'll never regret it. Please.

All my love, Dallas.

Annie's eyes began to mist. Damn him, anyway. Sending his dog to do his dirty work. He knew she couldn't resist Jet. She fell to her knees and hugged the wriggling dog. "I've missed you," she said, burrowing her face into his soft head. "I've missed you so much."

"What about me?"

A shadow crossed over her, and she looked up into Dallas's dark eyes. They were filled with remorse. Sorrow. And love.

"Dallas..."

"Hear me out, okay?"

"We've been through this."

"Please."

"All right. You want to go inside?"

"Dusty's there."

"Yeah. The two of you planned this, didn't you?"

"Guilty. But I want to talk to you privately, so we'll stay here." He sat down next to her on the stoop, picked up something shiny, and slipped it in his pocket. He took both of her hands in his large, beautiful ones. "If I could relive the last two weeks, I'd do so much differently, Annie."

She nodded. "So would I."

"Don't be silly. You didn't do anything wrong."

"I told you about the pill."

"And I should have let you explain. You should have been able to talk to me. Hell, you should be able to tell me anything. That's how it should be between two people who love each other."

"I never said—"

"I know you didn't. But I love you. And that's enough for now. You don't have to love me. All I ask is that you give me the chance to convince you I'm worth loving."

"You're worth loving, Dallas."

"I hope so. I can't change what's happened, but I can promise you I love you and I trust you. I know who you are. You're bright, and warm, and caring, and wonderful. There's not a deceptive bone in your body, and I think I knew that all the time. I won't let my experiences with Chelsea color our relationship ever again. I swear it. I'll do whatever you want to prove that. I'll even go to counseling."

Annie couldn't help giggling. Dallas McCray in counseling? "You do love me, don't you?"

"More than anything."

"I can't imagine you agreeing to counseling. You don't

seem the type."

"If it's what you want, I'll do it."

She sighed. "You don't need counseling, Cowboy. You need a good stiff kick in the shorts."

"I've gotten that. From Zach, Dusty, and Chad. Even from my ma." He chuckled. "From Jet, too. And the biggest came from myself."

Annie stared into his coffee-hued eyes. Could she forgive him? Oh, she wanted to. She wanted nothing more than to melt into his strong arms and live happily ever after.

"Riggs might come after me again."

"He won't. He's going to prison for a long time."

"For parole violation? And for beating me up? That's not likely to lead to a life sentence."

"But murder will."

"What?" Annie's body tensed. "What do you mean, murder?"

"I hired a private investigator. An old school chum of Chad's. The fella can track anything. It seems Riggs killed a convenience store clerk in Tiny Creek, Kansas."

"They're sure it's Riggs?"

"He's on videotape."

"Wow." Annie leaned back against her front door. "Wow."

"So he will go to prison for a long time."

"He could escape."

"Not likely. But if he did, I'd protect you. With my life if I had to."

"I don't want you in danger."

"I'm not. The only danger to me is a broken heart, Doc." He let go of her hands and pulled her into a hug. "God, I love you so damn much it hurts."

The ice around Annie's heart began to melt. She started to speak, but Dallas touched two fingers to her lips.

"There's something I need to say. And to be honest, I'm afraid to tell you."

"What is it?"

"I want to be completely honest with you. I want you to trust me, and I want you to understand that I trust you."

"Okay. That's what you wanted to tell me?"

"No."

"Then what?"

"Larry, he's the PI, found something else."

"Uh-huh?"

"I suppose you know Riggs didn't have the resources to find you on his own."

"I hadn't thought about it. Although he did want money from me. But then, he always wanted money."

"He had help finding you. The trail leads back to—"

"Oh God." Annie took a deep breath. "Chelsea."

"Yeah. And Jon Parker." Dallas reached toward Annie's face and twirled a stray curl around his fingers. "This is my fault, Annie. Not yours. I know you blame me."

"What Chelsea does is not your fault, Dallas."

"If I hadn't married her in the first place—"

"Then we wouldn't have met," Annie said.

"What?"

"Everything you do, every person who crosses your path, contributes to where you are today. Who you are today." She reached toward him, her hand shaking, and caressed his lightly stubbled cheek. "And who you are today is the man I love."

He pulled away from her, his gaze meeting hers. As Annie

looked into his eyes, she swore she saw straight into his soul.

"Say that again," he said. "Please." His chin trembled, and his emotion swirled into Annie as if it were her own.

"I love you, Dallas McCray. I have since that first night when you stayed with me and comforted me. I knew then there would never be anyone else."

"Oh, Annie. Baby." He pulled her into his body and took her mouth in a frantic meeting of lips and tongues. Annie's heart burst with the joy of his kiss. Of his love.

"Say you'll stay with me." Dallas nipped her earlobe and whispered against her skin. "Please. Say you'll stay."

"I'll stay, Cowboy." She pushed away slightly. "But you'd better never hurt me again."

"God. Never. I swear it. I never—"

"Make the same mistake twice," they finished in unison.

"Well, I don't," he said. He nibbled on her neck, his hands roaming over her breasts. "I want to take you to bed. Now."

Annie's pulse raced. "Here? On my stoop?"

"I could." He pressed her hand onto his arousal, which was very apparent through his jeans. "I don't even have to work up to it. I'm hard whenever I'm near you. Hell, I'm hard whenever I'm thinking of you, which is all the time. It's made me crazy."

"You'll have to wait a little while, Cowboy."

"Not long, I hope."

"No." She smiled into his eyes. "Not long."

"Oh"—Dallas scrounged in his pocket—"I almost forgot. I know it's soon and all, but since you're staying, and since you love me"—he winked—"I'd like to give you this."

In his hand was the most beautiful ring Annie had ever seen. Amethyst baguettes surrounded a large emerald cut diamond set in yellow gold.

"I never realized this before, but those purple stones match your eyes perfectly," Dallas said. "White gold or platinum would be better with your skin tone. We'll have it reset."

"Reset?"

"Yeah. I want it to be perfect for you."

"It is perfect, Dallas."

"It doesn't have to be an engagement ring. I know it's early. You can wear it on your right hand, and maybe someday, soon I hope, you'll want to wear it on your left."

"Dallas, I—"

"It was my grandmother's. My ma gave it to me when I turned twenty-one. I never gave it to Chelsea. It didn't feel right. But it feels exactly right to give it to you, Annie."

"Oh, Cowboy." Annie closed her eyes and two tears squeezed out and trickled down her cheeks.

"It's okay, Doc."

"Yes. It's very okay, and don't you dare have this ring reset, Dallas McCray. It's perfect as it is."

"All right. If that's what you want."

"It's what I want." She sniffed. "Well, aren't you going to put it on me?"

He smiled and took her right hand, but she pulled it away. "Wrong hand, Cowboy."

His eyes widened, the darkness sparkling. "You mean?"

"Yeah. Let's make it an engagement ring. If that's what you want."

"Oh, baby." He kissed her lips hard. "I'm going to be a gentleman and do this right. Stand up."

Annie rose and Dallas knelt before her, taking her left

hand in his. "Annalisa DeSimone, I love you with all my heart. Will you be my wife?"

Tears of joy flowed as Annie knelt down to face Dallas. "I love you too. Yes, I would be honored to be your wife."

Dallas slipped the ring onto Annie's finger. "A perfect fit." He smiled. "I knew it would be."

"Me too," Annie said. "A perfect fit."

Jet panted and wiggled around them. "How long did you make this poor dog sit out here on my stoop?"

"Long enough for Dusty to get you out the door."

"Tyrant." She clasped her hand to her mouth. "Oh my God. When I opened your note, something fell out. Was it...?"

"Yeah, it was the ring."

"You put an antique diamond ring around a dog's neck?"

"I'm no dummy. I know you can't resist Jet."

"You're no dummy?" Annie laughed. "I can see we're going to have to have a little talk about priceless objects and their care."

"I don't put much stock in things, Doc, although this ring does mean a lot to me, since it was my grandma's."

"I'll take excellent care of it," Annie said. "I promise never to put it around a dog's neck. In fact, I promise never to take it off."

"Then it will be exactly where it belongs." Dallas stood and pulled Annie to her feet. "And now I'm going to make love to you, my beautiful wife-to-be. I can't wait any longer. So go get rid of Dusty."

"I can't just kick her out."

"I can."

"Dallas!"

Annie stood helplessly on her stoop for less than a minute

before Dusty came rushing out.

Annie opened her mouth to speak, but Dusty shushed her. "Don't say a word. I understand completely." She pulled Annie into a hug. "I'm so happy for both of you. Bye."

When Annie entered the bedroom, Dallas was already lying on the bed. Naked. Her breath caught. She would never tire of the beautiful, magnificent sight of him. She undressed slowly and provocatively, purposefully tormenting him.

"You're killing me, Doc."

"I know. I love this power I have over you."

"Get your pretty self over here. Now."

"Ah. Exerting husbandly authority already, are we?"

When she had finally disrobed completely, he pulled her onto the bed. "I'm going to love you until dawn," he whispered.

Annie climbed on top of him and impaled herself, easing down slowly, the sweet stroke of him completing her. "Only until dawn, huh?" Her words were a breathless rasp. "I'm going to love you forever, Cowboy."

EPILOGUE

A Month Later

"She had the eye of every single man around." Chad clapped Dallas on the back and kissed the cheek of his new sister-in-law. "You're lucky you saw her first, big brother."

"I know," Dallas said, squeezing his wife's hand. "Believe me, I know."

The small wedding held at Laurie McCray's sprawling ranch house had turned into a lavish reception, complete with a champagne fountain and buffet dinner with a giant baron of McCray roast beef. Annie's parents had flown out and Sylvia and Laurie had become fast friends.

"Come dance with me, Chad."

Annie turned to see Caitlyn Bay, looking exquisite in a clingy dress of pink silk. Chad's eyes widened. Clearly he took notice of his pretty young neighbor.

"I'm not much of a dancer, Catie," he said.

"What a crock," Catie said. "You've danced with every woman here, including my mother and my sister. I want my turn."

"I don't think it would be appropriate."

Annie pulled Chad close and whispered, "Dance with her. It would mean a lot to her."

"She's just a kid, Annie."

"Dance with her anyway. It's my wedding. Do it for me."

"Christ. All right." He turned back to Catie and took her

arm. "Let's cut the rug, little bit."

Annie winced at the term *little bit*. "Lord, he's going to break her heart," she said to Dallas.

"Break her heart? She's a kid, Doc."

"She's seventeen, Cowboy. That's darn close to eighteen."

"Still a kid."

"Not according to your great State of Colorado. Or the United States, for that matter."

"And Chad's twenty-eight."

"So? Next year he'll be twenty-nine, and she'll be eighteen. Legal and all. She's in love with him, Dallas. Look at the stars in her eyes."

"Chad has more than enough women in love with him as it is. More than even *he* can handle, and they're all over twenty-one. Catie's just a friend of the family."

"You are blind as a bat. She's in love."

"If it's anything, it's just a crush."

"Husband, you are so naive."

His lazy grin started her heart racing. "I like it when you say that."

"That you're naive?"

He cupped her cheek in his hand. "Nah. When you call me *husband*."

"Ah. In that case, husband, husband, husband. My gorgeous, rugged, incredible husband. Would you do something for me?"

"Anything. I'm at your command."

"Oh, I like that."

"I figured you would. What's your wish, baby? I'll do anything for you."

"Would you take me to bed?"

"Annie, honey?"

"What?"

"Let me make this perfectly clear." He picked her up and headed toward the house. "The answer to that question will always be a resounding yes."

"Geez, Cowboy, not in front of all these people." She struggled, giggling, but didn't put much fight into it. "I meant later. At home."

"Don't want to wait."

"What's your mother going to think?"

"Don't care."

"What's *my* mother going to think?"

"Still don't care."

"In that case"—she smiled into his warm brown eyes, dark with desire—"hurry."

CONTINUE THE TEMPTATION SAGA WITH
BOOK THREE

Taking

CATIE

Available Now
Keep reading for an excerpt!

CHAPTER ONE

Chad McCray loved women. Brunette, blond, or redhead, thin and willowy or curvy and voluptuous, he adored them all. Exploring their bodies and sating his sexual hunger was his favorite hobby.

Yes, he did adore women.

Commitment?

Not so much.

Since women seemed to love him as well, life had been good for his thirty-two years. In his two decades of loving the fairer sex, only one had tried badgering him into commitment. He'd gotten rid of her faster than a bucking bronc tosses a cowpoke. Now, he was on his way out the door to pick up a new luscious lollipop he'd met at a community potluck. Light blond hair, cherry-red lips, and curves that went on forever—Amber Cross, the new manicurist in town, was a tasty treat he looked forward to sampling.

The ring of his cell phone interrupted his lascivious thoughts. He scooped it out of his pocket and stared at the screen. His brother Zach.

"What's up, Zach?"

"Got an opportunity of a lifetime for you, Chad," Zach's deep voice said.

"What might that be?"

"Well, it seems you, Dallas, and I have been chosen to judge the rodeo queen contest this year."

Chad guffawed into the phone. "You mean Dusty and Annie are going to let you and Dallas ogle the cheesecake of Bakersville? You've got to be kidding." The mere thought of his disgustingly happily married brothers judging a beauty pageant brought a smirk to his lips. "I, on the other hand, would be honored."

Zach chuckled. "Our wives trust us. We're committed."

"Should *be* committed, you mean." Chad checked his watch. "Do you need anything else at the moment? I'm due to meet a lovely little cream puff in half an hour."

"Meet her? You mean you're not picking her up at her place?"

"Nope. We're meeting at the Bullfrog for a drink."

"One day, little brother," Zach said, "you're going to meet a woman who knocks your boots right off. A woman you want to treat like a lady."

"Not likely," Chad said. "My life is pretty darn perfect the way it is. When I need a home cooked meal, I crash your house or Dallas's. And when I want a critter fix, I have Sean and the twins. All the family love, but none of the responsibility. That's the way I like it."

"Sean's my critter, and the twins are Dallas's." Zach's tone turned serious. "Don't you want one of your own? You're not getting any younger, you know."

"Worried about my biological clock, Zach?" Chad laughed.

"Nope," his brother said. "Just worried you're going to wake up one day and find yourself alone."

Chad smiled, imagining the sweet red lips of Miss Amber Cross roaming over every inch of his body. "One thing I can guarantee you, brother. I'll never be alone."

★ ★ ★

Caitlyn Bay ran into her brother's arms at baggage claim in Denver. Fatigued and dehydrated from the trip from Paris, she looked a mess.

"Hey, Catie-bug," Harper said, kissing the top of her head. He pushed her away. "Let me look at you. You're all grown up."

"You just saw me in Brussels at Christmas, Harper," Catie said, "and right now I'm a fright."

"Nonsense, you're gorgeous as always. People at home aren't even going to recognize you. You left four years ago a freckle-faced girl in ponytails, and now you're a chic Parisian grad student." He shook his head. "I still don't know why you never came home for the holidays." He steadied her as she stumbled. "And still a notorious klutz."

Catie ignored the jibe. "You know why. I wanted to travel, to see the world. And I did, Harp. I saw it all."

"I think you stayed away to avoid a certain cowboy by the name of McCray," Harper said. "Chad's still single, you know."

Catie looked away. "My bags here yet?"

"Your plane just got in, honey. Your bags'll be a few minutes. Nice save, by the way."

"What do you mean?" she asked innocently. Inside, her heart was thumping like the hooves of a racehorse at the thought of Chad McCray.

"He's damn near twice your age, Catie."

"I have no interest in Chad McCray. And he hasn't been twice my age since I was eleven and he was twenty-two. Even so, I happen to be twenty-one years old now, as you well know. Legal and everything. I can even order a margarita when I want one. In fact, I think I want one now."

"Now?"

"Heck, yeah. I'm exhausted, and my brain is fried. I can't think of a better salve for myself at the moment. Mind if we stop at the Bullfrog on the way home?"

"I think you've lost your mind, little sis. You've never set foot in the Bullfrog."

"Because I haven't been able to. Legally. But now I can. I want my big brother to buy me my first legal drink."

"You've been drinking in France for four years."

Catie gave her brother a friendly swat. "You make it sound like I'm some kind of a lush. You know I hardly ever indulge. But right now a little lime and tequila sounds thirst-quenching good. You can't get a Colorado margarita in Paris, Harp."

"Even with all that Grand Marnier and Cointreau they got there?" Harper's handsome face twisted into a teasing grin.

"Give me plain old Triple Sec and Cuervo any day," Catie said. "And I can't wait to sink my teeth into some Colorado Angus. French food is wonderful, but I sure have missed Colorado cuisine."

"Ma's got a big homecoming planned at the house tomorrow night," Harper said. "Everyone shy of Murphy'll be there"—he winked—"including Chad McCray."

"I couldn't give two puny figs," Catie said, avoiding her brother's gaze.

Her words came out strong, with a huff and a scorn.

But they were one big ol' lie.

★ ★ ★

The Bullfrog Lounge featured live music and the best

margaritas outside of Mexico. Or so the sign said. Mostly what the bar featured was a crowded dance floor that forced couples to mesh together whether the music was fast or slow. This suited Chad just fine. Miss Amber Cross was as gorgeous as he remembered, and tonight a tight denim skirt hugged those narrow hips like a snakeskin. Her bodacious breasts nearly poured out of her snug cotton tank top, and her platinum waves settled nicely over her sleek golden shoulders. Lips as red and full as he remembered, and he'd already had the pleasure of sampling them while they sat at the bar sipping their drinks. Another drink, a few more close dances, and he figured she'd be ready to hit the sack.

"What are you thinking about, cowboy?" Amber asked, as Chad led her back to their seats at the bar.

"Thinking another drink might be in order, honey."

Amber sat down on her bar stool and crossed her creamy thighs. "That dancing did make me thirsty."

"What'll it be this time?"

"Same thing. A cosmo, I think."

Chad chuckled under his breath. Those girly drinks did nothing for him. His brothers favored scotch and bourbon, but Chad was a beer man all the way. "One cosmo for the lady," he told the bartender, "and another Fat Tire for me." Chad threw a twenty on the counter. "Keep the change."

"So tell me more about the infamous McCray brothers," Amber said. "I've heard lots, but being new here, I'm not sure what's gossip and innuendo and what's truth."

Chad let out a boisterous laugh. "Honey, it's all gossip here in Bakersville. It's a small town, and everybody knows everybody else's business. What exactly have you heard?"

"Just that you all are the richest men in town, owners of

the largest ranch. And you all love the ladies." Her sweet lips curved in to a flirtatious grin.

"Honey, my big brothers are both married. Lovesick as they come."

"Oh? Are they as fine looking as you are, Chad?"

"Some say finer." Chad winked. "Dallas, he's the oldest, is married to Annie, the vet here in town. They have twin girls, Sylvie and Laurie, named after their grandmas. And Zach, he's the middle brother, is married to a sweet little girl we've known since we were kids. He and Dusty have a four-year-old boy, Sean."

"And your parents? They still around?"

"My pa died nearly ten years ago and my ma just last year."

"Goodness. I'm sorry. I didn't mean to bring up bad memories."

"It's okay, honey. My ma had aggressive breast cancer. By the time she was diagnosed, the docs only gave her a year to live. She made it two. We consider that good fortune."

"Wow." Amber took a sip of the cocktail the bartender set in front of her. "I'm real sorry. That's tough."

"It was, but we're fine. We're muddling through. My brothers have their families, and they take good care of me."

"Meaning?"

"Meaning, I can crash with them when I need some family time. Mostly I hang at my own place, though. And speaking of my place"—he took her hand and rubbed his calloused thumb over her smooth manicured fingers—"I've got the makings for more cosmos there. And the sweetest black lab you'd ever want to meet."

"Oh, I love dogs," Amber gushed.

"Marnie'd love to meet you, honey," he said, circling his thumb in her palm. A little hand massage always sent the right message.

"You have remarkable hands," Amber said, closing her eyes. "Ever think of going into the nail business?" She let out a girlish giggle.

"Can't say I have, honey," Chad said. "My ranch keeps me pretty darn busy."

"Mmm. Well, you sure know how to give a good hand massage. Come by the shop sometime, and I'll return the favor. No charge."

"I've got a better idea." He dropped her hand and ran his fingers up the smooth silk or her arms and shoulders.

"What's that?"

"How about you give me that massage tonight?" He leaned over and kissed her lips lightly. "At my place."

"You are just one sweet-talking cowboy, aren't you, Chad McCray?"

"Is that a yes?"

"What must you think of me? Barely in town a month and going home with a man I hardly know."

"I think we're attracted to each other. What's wrong with that? As for barely knowing me—" He trailed his lips to her ear and nipped her lobe. "I guarantee you by morning we'll know each other a whole heckuva lot better."

She shuddered under his mouth, and he smiled against her cheek. Bingo.

"Sure, it sounds fun," Amber said. "Let's go."

Chad chugged the last of his beer, took Amber's hand to lead her to the door of the bar, and ran smack dab into his neighbor Harper Bay.

"Watch where you're going, Bay," he said jovially. "You damn near knocked me off my feet."

"Hey, Chad," Harper said, "who do you have there?"

"This is Amber. She's working for Judy at the beauty shop. Amber, Harper Bay. He runs the ranch next to ours."

"Nice to meet you."

"A pleasure," Harper said, taking Amber's hand. "Can you hold on a minute, there's someone I know would like to see you."

"Who?"

"Give her a minute," Harper said. "She went to freshen up."

"Her?" Chad's brain churned. Who would Harper have with him? He looked toward the ladies room, and within ten seconds, a goddess emerged. Tall and sleek, with mahogany hair that drifted past her shoulders in silky waves and a face that could rival Helen of Troy in beauty. And a body...breasts as luscious as any, curvy hips, and long legs that went on forever in those clingy jeans. Who the hell was she?

Harper turned and grabbed the woman's hand. "You remember Catie, don't you, Chad?"

Chad's stomach dropped, as did his jaw. This was Catie Bay? Little Catie Bay, who used to wear her brown hair in pigtails and spent her life in the barn with her horses?

Had she always had breasts?

Where were the freckles? The braids? The...little girl? Where was the damn little girl? That little girl had nursed a mega-crush on Chad growing up. He and his brothers had always known. Ever since he'd been paired up with Catie's older sister, Angelina, for a project in high school and he'd spent massive time at the Bay ranch. Catie'd been four then and had followed Chad around like a lovesick pup. Damn, she'd been a cute little thing. He'd seen her a lot over the years, watched her grow up. Hell, he'd danced with her at Dallas's wedding. She wasn't more than seventeen at the time, and he'd been, what? Twenty-eight or so? She'd been turning into a pretty thing then, but she was still a kid.

Then another image flashed through Chad's mind—the last time he'd seen Catie Bay. At her eighteenth birthday party, some four years ago now. She'd cornered him in the private gazebo at her ranch, and...

His groin tightened.

He was eleven years her senior, and he'd stopped it. But it had been damn near the hardest thing he'd ever done. He remembered luscious eighteen-year-old lips clambering to touch his. Perky eighteen-year-old nipples poking through her silky green dress. Damn, she'd looked good in green, but she was a kid. Still had a light spray of freckles across her nose...

This woman standing next to Harper was no kid.

Nope, no kid at all.

MESSAGE FROM HELEN HARDT

Dear Reader,

Thank you for reading *Teasing Annie*. If you want to find out about my current backlist and future releases, please like my Facebook page: **www.facebook.com/HelenHardt** and join my mailing list: **www.helenhardt.com/signup/**. I often do giveaways. If you're a fan and would like to join my street team to help spread the word about my books, you can do so here: **www.facebook.com/groups/hardtandsoul/**. I regularly do awesome giveaways for my street team members.

If you enjoyed the story, please take the time to leave a review on a site like Amazon or Goodreads. I welcome all feedback.

I wish you all the best!

Helen

ALSO BY HELEN HARDT

The Sex and the Season Series:
Lily and the Duke
Rose in Bloom
Lady Alexandra's Lover
Sophie's Voice
The Perils of Patricia (Coming Soon)

The Temptation Saga:
Tempting Dusty
Teasing Annie
Taking Catie
Taming Angelina
Treasuring Amber
Trusting Sydney
Tantalizing Maria

The Steel Brothers Saga:
Craving
Obsession
Possession
Melt (Coming December 20th, 2016)
Burn (Coming February 14th, 2017)
Surrender (Coming May 16th, 2017)

Daughters of the Prairie:
The Outlaw's Angel
Lessons of the Heart
Song of the Raven

ACKNOWLEDGMENTS

Teasing Annie (formerly *A Cowboy and a Gentleman*) is the second book in the *Temptation Saga*. It won second place in the RomCon Readers' Crown contest in 2012, beaten by its prequel, *Tempting Dusty.*

So many people helped along the way in bringing this book to you. Celina Summers, Michele Hamner Moore, Jenny Rarden, Coreen Montagna, Ruth Horvath, Kelly Shorten, David Grishman, Meredith Wild, Jonathan Mac, Kurt Vachon, Yvonne Ellis, Shayla Fereshetian—thank you all for your expertise and guidance. Eternal thanks to Waterhouse Press for the expert rebranding of the series. Waterhouse rocks!

And thanks most of all to you, the readers. I hope you love Dallas and Annie's story. Up next is the youngest McCray brother, Chad, who sees a girl from a neighboring ranch in a different light. Don't miss *Taking Catie.*

ABOUT THE AUTHOR

New York Times and *USA Today* Bestselling author Helen Hardt's passion for the written word began with the books her mother read to her at bedtime. She wrote her first story at age six and hasn't stopped since. In addition to being an award winning author of contemporary and historical romance and erotica, she's a mother, a black belt in Taekwondo, a grammar geek, an appreciator of fine red wine, and a lover of Ben and Jerry's ice cream. She writes from her home in Colorado, where she lives with her family. Helen loves to hear from readers.

Visit her here:
www.facebook.com/HelenHardt

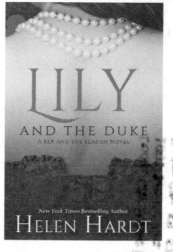